FIREWALL

JESSICA MEHRING

5 PRINCE PUBLISHING

Published by 5 PRINCE PUBLISHING & BOOKS, LLC

PO Box 865, Arvada, CO 80001

www.5PrinceBooks.com

ISBN digital: 978-1-63112-321-4

ISBN print: 978-1-63112-322-1

Cover Credit: Marianne Nowicki

070502023

To the heroes of Colorado Springs Fire Station 16.
I will forever be in your debt.

Acknowledgments

The author career attracts introverts like me because, from the outside, it appears to be a solitary pursuit. The reality is, though, that writing a book is a team sport.

Bernadette Soehner, you believed in me from the start, and you gave me a safe space to stretch my wings.

Cate Byers, you pushed me kindly and laughed in all the right places as you edited this manuscript.

Jeremy, Autumn, and Cassie, you supported and encouraged me every step of the way, even as I kicked you out of the room so I could get my writing done.

Nina, our weekly coffee and hiking dates kept me from feeling like I was living in a cave as I wrote this book on nights and weekends.

Finally, Mom and Dad, your pride in me means more than you know.

ALSO BY JESSICA MEHRING

A Rocky Mountain Romance

Firewall

FIREWALL

ONE

VERONICA

VERONICA CLARK PUT HER BLACK KITTEN HEELS UP ON her desk, gazed out over the San Francisco skyline, and nudged her earbuds into her ears as she dialed Cara's number. As the call rang through, she took a deep breath and enjoyed the view. She couldn't quite see San Francisco Bay—there were too many towers in the Financial District between her and the water—but she could feel in her bones the call of the saltwater.

"Tell me you're not working late," Cara said on the other end of the line without even a hello.

Veronica laughed. "I don't plan on it. Just have a few more things to finish up, and my weekend can officially begin." *And I can finally get out to Ocean Beach for some surfing tomorrow.*

"That's what I like to hear. I've got one more class to teach, and I'm ready to party. Let's kick it off with martinis at Largo's. Six o'clock?"

Veronica frowned. "It's been a long week, I'm not really up for socializing."

"You say that every weekend," Cara said. "And every weekend, I drag you out with me, and we have fun. Stop arguing."

Veronica could practically hear Cara's eyes rolling when she spoke. "Fine," She sighed. "It'll take me about an hour to get home, get changed, and catch a ride. Let's make it six thirty, just to be safe."

"You can just go to the bar looking like an FBI agent. There's nothing wrong with that," Cara chided.

"Says the schoolmarm." Veronica laughed. "Besides, I don't look like an agent. I look like a high-end lawyer. Get it right."

"At least we clean up nice," Cara said. "Did I tell you that Angus came to our family dinner with a big streak of soot on his face last Saturday?"

"Teacher, firefighter—your family is like a Norman Rockwell painting. I'm sure even the sooty face was endearing."

"I wish this was a video call so you could see just how much I'm rolling my eyes right now."

"Save the attitude for your history students. I'll see you tonight. Later, skater." Veronica smiled and hit the end-call button. She took a deep breath and stared out the window. It was mid-afternoon on a sunny September day, and the sun was high overhead, giving the city an angelic glow. The autumn season made Veronica miss sunny San Diego. This was the best time of year for good weather in San Francisco—but these sunny days were the norm back home.

Veronica was all smiles when she hung up the phone—but it didn't last long. She heard the door open behind her, and she spun in her chair knowing she'd be face-to-face with Sunset Financial CEO Craig Truman. He was the only person at the company who would dare walk into her office without knocking.

"What's this request for data isolation software?" he demanded, throwing a piece of paper down on Veronica's glass desk.

Without looking at the paper, she answered, "We need a data vault."

"Why?" he growled.

"So hackers won't steal our data."

"Isn't it your job to make sure hackers can't steal our data? Should I replace you with a...whatever you just called it?"

"Data vault. For isolating data. It keeps hackers from accessing, stealing, and selling Sunset's data. Pretty straightforward. We don't have one. We need one. I talked that company into a good deal." Veronica put her index finger on the paper on her desk and pushed it toward Craig.

"It's too expensive."

"Compared to the cost of paying cybercriminals a ransom to get *some* of Sunset's data back? It's a steal."

"Did Devon sign off on this?"

"Devon is the only one who could have approved the purchase order you're holding in your hands." Veronica leaned back in her chair and crossed her legs. "What's the problem, Craig? This is necessary for the security of the company. The CFO approved the purchase. I don't understand why you're so worked up."

"In the three years you've been here, our spending on information security has tripled. Newman sang your praises when he hired you, but he's gone now, and Travis and I don't like where our spending is heading."

Travis. That answers the question. Veronica sat forward, and a lock of blonde hair escaped her neat bun. She tucked it behind her ear. "Let me ask you this. Has Sunset been in the news for any data breaches in the last three years?"

Craig hesitated. "No."

"What about your competitors? Have you seen them in the news for data breaches?"

Craig's frown deepened. "Yes."

Veronica smiled serenely. "You're welcome. And you can tell Travis that my *in-budget* spending is what's keeping him in his cushy new chief technology officer role. His head would be on the chopping block—and so would yours—if we had a breach."

A knock on the door made them both turn. One of the wealth

managers from the third floor was standing in the doorway. "Sorry
to interrupt," he said, his face turning red as he recognized the
CEO. "Veronica, we're getting server timeouts, and Gary and Boyd
are both out today. Can you come take a look?"

Veronica stood and smoothed her fitted black blazer. "That's
my cue. Have a good weekend, Craig." She nodded at him as she
passed, and resisted the urge to slam her office door behind her.

The wealth manager kept pace with her as she walked down
the long, cubicle-lined hall toward the elevators. "You're braver
than I am," he said in a hushed tone.

"Why do you say that?" Veronica raised an eyebrow in his
direction.

"Every time I'm in his presence, I feel like he's going to fire me
on a whim. How can you be so calm?"

"I surf," Veronica said with a laugh. "It's hard to feel anxious
about anything after a few hours out on the water."

The wealth manager shivered. "Surfing in these icy waters? So
that's it. You're just a glutton for punishment."

They came to a stop at the elevators and she turned to him
with a sly grin. "I like a challenge," she said, pushing the button to
go down. "Also, it helps that this isn't the only job in the world for
someone with my skills and experience."

As they stepped into the elevator, Veronica felt the wealth
manager's eyes on her.

"Are you...interviewing?" he whispered, nervously glancing
around as if he were looking for cameras.

"Let's just say I've always got a backup plan," she answered
with a wink. *And the standing offer at Pacific Wealth
Management doesn't hurt my confidence, either.* As the elevator
descended, she turned that offer over in her mind. It would be a
good gig. But she'd have to commute or move to Daly City, and
she'd come to love living in San Francisco. Especially since she met
her best friend, Cara. It was Cara who brought her out of the shell

she'd been in since her dad died, and it was Cara who had taught her how to find joy on dry land. She owed her too much to up and move away. *Better to stick it out here and deal with Craig's growing ego. Besides, the Pacific job isn't going anywhere.*

TWO

ANGUS

ANGUS MILLER COMPLETED HIS LAST PULL-UP, DROPPED to the floor, and mopped the sweat from his brow. The small on-site gym at Fire Station 62 was empty except for one other man, who was currently hogging the leg press.

"Marcel, you gonna get done sometime today?" Angus chided between sips from his water bottle.

"Sorry, boss," Marcel replied with a rounded Louisiana accent. "One more set and it's all yours."

Angus shook his head and smiled. "No worries, man. I'm just in a hurry to get this workout over with. My father and my grandfather always told me that being a firefighter was a physically demanding job. What they neglected to tell me is that I'd have to work so hard to be fit enough to work so hard." He set his water bottle down on a nearby table and ran his fingers through his damp hair. *I need a haircut*, he thought as he caught a glimpse of himself and his too-long black hair in the mirrored wall. It wasn't quite to the length where it was getting in his eyes, but it was too close.

Marcel grunted as he gave the leg press one last thrust before locking the weights in place. "All yours, boss," he said as he got out of the machine. "Hey, didn't you just finish your tour this morning? Why are you here and not out enjoying a beer in the sunshine?"

Angus shrugged. "You know what they say. Never skip leg day."

Marcel laughed, then gave a backward wave as he left the room.

Angus wiped down the bench and then slid his body into place. He always left the leg press for last. Out of all the exercises he did on a regular basis, this felt like the most important one. With strong legs, he could climb a ladder to save someone on an upper floor, he could haul the heavy equipment needed to put out the flames, and he could safely carry someone from a fire. All the other muscle groups mattered, too, of course, but his legs were his foundation.

Halfway through the second set, he heard his cell phone ring across the room. The ringtone was La Cucaracha, which meant that it was his sister calling. He sighed. He was in no hurry to find out what she wanted. Lately Cara had been on a mission to fix him up with friends of hers from work, and he had no time for that nonsense. Angus was fully focused on becoming battalion chief before the year was out. If he succeeded, he'd be the youngest man in his family to achieve that rank.

Angus set the weights in place and slid out from the leg press machine. He wiped his face with his exercise towel, then meandered over to his gym bag to pack up. Finally, when he couldn't find a reason to delay any longer, he pulled his phone out of the bag's side pocket and clicked the button to listen to his voicemail.

"Angus, it's your sister. My friend Veronica and I are going out for drinks tonight—she's the techie one, and no, I'm not trying to set you up, so stop fuming."

Angus snorted.

"I just promised Aunt Katie that I'd check on her cats while she's gone back to Ireland for the month, and I don't think you know how hard it is to get Veronica to commit to being social—of course you don't know, you've never met her, because you're just as anti-social as she is—but anyway, brother, will you pleeease check on Katie's cats for me tonight? I'll owe you a big one! Text me back. I know it's too much to ask you to call me back."

Smiling at the phone, Angus clicked the button to end the voicemail. Cara may be annoying, but she can be pretty charming too. He never could say no when she rambled at him like that. He pulled up the text message app and wrote his response. "YOU OWE ME BIG."

As Angus walked through the firehouse on his way out, he heard the sound of a TV coming from the shared living room and decided to make a pit stop. He poked his head in the door and found Marcel and two other firefighters watching the news. "Anything interesting happening in the world?" he asked no one in particular.

Marcel turned to look at him, then shook his head. "Go home, boss. Or at least, get out of here. You've got four days of freedom before your next shift—don't waste them here with us." He nodded toward the two men stretched out in matching leather recliners. "Besides, Thatcher and Greer stink to high heaven."

When the two men didn't respond, Marcel and Angus burst out laughing.

"Fine. See you on the next tour," Angus said as he walked out of the room.

The afternoon sunlight was blinding after being inside for the last hour. Angus slipped on his sunglasses and breathed in the lightly salty air the wind had brought in as it had pushed out the clouds earlier in the day.

He never quite knew what to do with himself on his days off. At least feeding Aunt Katie's cats meant he didn't have to go back to his empty apartment or fend off dinner invitations from his well-meaning parents.

Angus walked up the block to where he had parked his green

Toyota 4Runner, and climbed into the driver's seat. *Maybe I'll go for a run after I feed the cats. Then get some Thai food...* A text message notification interrupted his thoughts.

"THANKS BROTHER," read the message from Cara. It was immediately followed by another message. "BTW, DAD GOT A NEW TV AND HE WANTS YOUR HELP GETTING THE STREAMING APPS SET UP ON IT. BEWARE."

Angus turned off the ringer on his phone, then pulled out onto the street and headed north to Union Square.

THREE
VERONICA

VERONICA HADN'T SPENT MORE THAN FIVE MINUTES ON the third floor before she knew the problem wasn't with the wealth managers' software. As she stepped off the elevator into the dry cold of the tower basement, her mind ran through every possible scenario—but the best place to start troubleshooting would be in the server room.

"Hey Martin," she greeted the security guard on duty.

He nodded at her, his feet still propped on the metal desk as he gave her badge a brief courtesy check. "Veronica. Nice to see you here in the dungeon. How's the weather up there?"

Veronica swiped her badge on the electronic pad next to the solid steel door, and looked sideways at the guard. "Terrible. It's bright and sunny."

The guard snorted. "Sounds awful."

"It is, when you have to be trapped indoors all day. I always pray for terrible weather on workdays. Don't you?" Veronica winked, then turned the handle and walked through the unlocked door.

The server room was cavernous and dark. What little light there was came from fluorescent bulbs overhead and blinking server lights all around. A few years into the job, now, she knew to always bring a flashlight and a headlamp. Years ago, when she was first hired for this role, she brought an IT support technician down with her to hold the flashlight. His yammering was so distracting, it took her twice as long as it should have to diagnose the problem. She quickly realized it's much more efficient just to do things herself.

Veronica surveyed the rows of servers, one by one. The lights blinked on and off in a complex pattern that would appear random to a layman—but she knew their dance. In the third row, toward the back, however, one of the lights had fallen out of step. It wasn't something even other IT professionals would have noticed, but to her, it was like watching the waves from the beach, and noticing that one wave was moving backward. It stuck out in the ordinary flow.

"What have we got here?" Veronica whispered to herself. She made her way to the rack and felt along the upper bezel of the middle server in the stack. As her fingers slid down to the lower bezel, she felt something odd. The bezel was slightly loose, leaving a tiny bit of unexpected space between it and the chassis that surrounded the machine's inner workings.

Veronica unzipped the tool kit she had brought with her, and the sound echoed through the server room. She pulled out a slim screwdriver and unscrewed the lower bezel. Setting the bezel on the floor, she pointed her flashlight into the machine and huffed. *Nothing strange here. Larry must have just not tightened the bezel the last time he worked on this one.*

When she went to place the bezel back on the chassis, that's when she saw it. A glint of metal on the hard disk drive where no shiny metal should be.

Veronica pointed the flashlight at the offending glint, and gently prodded at the metal piece with her screwdriver. It didn't budge. She pulled out a larger screwdriver from her kit, and unscrewed the hard drive from its housing. When it was free of its screws, she guided it out of the machine. Holding it at eye level, she squinted at the anomaly. *What have we here?*

The sudden sound of a fire alarm startled her, and she almost dropped the hard drive. Heart racing, Veronica fumbled with her tools, shoving them back into her kit. In her panic, she threw the hard drive in with the screwdrivers, then quickly made her way back to the door.

The security guard was just opening the stairwell door across the small guard room when she exited the server room. He jerked his chin toward the stairs. "Not sure if it's a drill or a real alarm, so use the stairs. I'll be right behind you after I lock up," he said as Veronica approached. She nodded her response and entered the dim stairwell, her heart still thudding in her chest.

Veronica had only made it to the first landing when the lights went out. "Shit," she said, feeling for the kit that she had slung over her shoulder. She unzipped it and found the flashlight by feel.

Something hit her hand hard, sending her flashlight flying. "What the..." She noticed the smell of cologne just before something shoved her from behind. She flung her arm out instinctively, and by a miracle, her hand landed on the railing. She grabbed a hold and stopped herself from falling down the stairs.

The emergency lights came on in the stairwell, just in time for her to see the silhouette of a person running up the stairs ahead of her.

Shaking, Veronica climbed the stairs to the first floor. When she exited the stairwell into the bright lobby, she had never been so happy to see sunlight.

Four

Angus

Angus's aunt Katie had three cats—none of which he liked, and none of which particularly liked him. But when he let himself into her apartment on the edge of Union Square, those cats rushed to him like he was an open can of tuna.

"Well, nice to see you, too," he said as the three felines wound around his legs and purred. The fat orange one—Sherbet, he thought—stood on its hind legs and kneaded Angus's pants with its front paws. "Ouch. Watch those claws, buddy."

Angus flipped on the light in the dim living room and immediately saw why the cats were so happy to see him. They were completely out of food and water. *I wonder if Cara realizes that cats need to be fed daily.* He found the bag of dry food in the kitchen cupboard where Cara had said it would be, and deftly filled the bowls. The cats wasted no time starting on their meals.

As Angus filled the cats' water dishes in the kitchen sink, he heard yelling from the street below. Even at six-foot-one, he had to stand on his tip-toes to see what was happening out the window over the sink. The people making all the racket seemed to be right up against the building. As far as he could tell, it was two men and two women arguing loudly, but he couldn't understand what they were saying.

His mild curiosity was immediately replaced by the urge to intervene when one of the men pulled a knife.

Angus was out the door and down the stairs in seconds. When he slammed open the front door of the apartment building, he didn't hesitate even long enough to get his bearings—he ran straight at the bald man he had seen with a knife outside the window. The two women screamed, the man with the knife yelled in a language Angus didn't recognize, and the other man held his hands in the air. The scene was chaos, but that's when things get clearest for a firefighter. That's when the rest of the world drops away and the only thing that matters is the situation at hand.

Barreling at the bald man, Angus dodged the edge of the blade, then hit the outside of the man's elbow hard to knock him off balance. Before the bald man could take another swipe at him, Angus slammed the heel of his hand into the man's nose. The bald man dropped to the ground. It had been an instinctive move, but Angus instantly regretted it—because while effective, it could also be fatal.

Angus knelt down and felt the bald man's neck for a pulse. It was faint, but it was there. He looked up and saw the other man running away. The two women, one brunette and one redhead, clung to each other and babbled in the same language the bald man had been speaking.

"Do you speak English?" he asked the women, trying to keep his voice calm.

They looked at him blankly for a moment, then shook their heads.

"I'm going to call the police," he said, miming a phone call with his hand to his ear.

They continued to stare, but didn't make a move to leave.

The redhead spoke up, but Angus couldn't understand what

she was saying. She pointed at the man on the ground and repeated the same phrase again and again, her eyes pleading for understanding.

"I'm sorry. I don't understand what you're saying," Angus said. He stood facing them with his palms open, trying to appear as nonthreatening as he could to these terrified women. "I will be right back. Stay here," he said, holding a finger up. As Angus ran back up to his aunt's apartment to get his cell phone, he hoped they were still there when he returned—but he wasn't holding his breath.

In less than two minutes, Angus returned with his cell phone. Sure enough, the women weren't there—and the only indication that there had been a man lying on the ground was a small puddle of blood on the sidewalk. *How in the world...That guy was out cold.* Angus ran his fingers through his hair and stared down the steep street that led toward the bay.

The wailing sound of a fire engine pulled his attention away from the mystery of the missing bald man. Seconds after the first truck raced past, two more followed in its wake. Angus knew better than to try to call his crew to find out what was going on. Engine Company 62 was near enough to his aunt's apartment that they were likely called in for whatever was going on—and none of his crew would be picking up their cell phone while they were on their way to the scene. So he did the next best thing and pulled up the social media feed for his local news station on his phone.

The only information Angus could glean from the newsfeed was that there was a tower on fire in the Financial District—not far from where his sister Cara lived. He dialed her number, and after four rings, it went to voicemail.

Angus didn't even bother checking to make sure his aunt's apartment was locked before he jumped in his 4Runner and headed toward the Financial District.

"CALL ME BACK, CARA. DAMMIT." ANGUS WAS TALKING to himself as he drove toward the fire, but he was also hoping that if there was a higher power listening, they'd pass on the message to her. Cara may be a giant pain in his rear, but she was still his baby sister.

As Angus guided his 4Runner east through the deliriously steep streets of San Francisco, he began to hear sirens coming from the direction of Market Street. Traffic was backed up for half a mile, and he knew he wouldn't get any closer by car. After circling a couple of blocks, he found a parking spot and pulled the SUV into it.

Angus might be slower on foot, but outside his vehicle he was able to use all his senses. The noise wasn't deafening, so whatever was happening was likely not a terrorist attack. The smoke smell in the air was faint, indicating the fire was contained. And most importantly, no one on the street looked panicked.

Turning onto Market Street, Angus stopped and looked east through the chasm of towers. The street was blocked off, and several fire trucks were parked in a row. The activity seemed to be centered on a building on the edge of Mechanics Monument Plaza.

Just as Angus took a step toward the commotion, his phone rang in his pocket. The caller ID showed Cara's name, and his heart did a backflip as he answered the phone. "You alright?" he said, relief making him sound out of breath.

"I'm fine. Why wouldn't I be?" Cara said. "What's going on?"

"There's a fire near your place."

"Well that explains why my bus is stopped dead in traffic."

"Why didn't you pick up your phone?"

"I had an administrative meeting after school, and my phone was still turned off."

"You scared me."

"You'll live. Where's the fire, anyway?"

"Near Market and First, I think. There's no one out on the

street, so it must be in one of the towers. I was walking toward it when you called."

The line went quiet for a moment before Cara finally responded. "It's not Sunset Financial Tower, is it?"

"I'm not sure."

"Well go make sure!" Cara's voice lost its comedic edge and became tinged with fear. "That's where Veronica works."

Angus noticed two firefighters walking toward one of the engines parked on Market Street. "Let me call you back," he said, hanging up before his sister could protest. He jogged across the empty street and approached the men, recognizing one of them almost instantly. "Taylor!" he said loudly, waving.

Taylor looked up and waved back, while the other man climbed up into the cab of the fire truck. Taylor's brown hair was plastered against his head in the front, and he held his black helmet against his side. "Hey, man. Long time."

Angus nodded. "I take it Ohio couldn't handle you."

Taylor shrugged, "I lasted two months in Cincinnati before the Bay Area called me home."

"This place is like a magnet. I get it." Angus noticed that Taylor's black turnout coat was pristine. "So—what's happening here?" He jerked his chin in the direction the two firefighters had come from.

"Fire at Sunset Financial Tower. Weirdest thing. Looked like someone had set fire to a box of paper in the stairwell."

Angus frowned. "That *is* weird. Any major damage? Injuries?"

Taylor shook his head. "Just a lot of wasted resources putting out a little bonfire in a concrete stairwell. It was extinguished before the tenants were even able to evacuate."

"Well, I'm glad no one was injured, at least. My sister is freaking out. One of her good friends works in the building."

A mischievous grin spread across Taylor's face. "How is Cara these days?"

Angus glared. "She's married," he lied. "Nice to run into you, Taylor. See you around." With that, he turned and walked back toward his car to call Cara and fill her in.

FIVE
VERONICA

VERONICA WAS ONE OF HUNDREDS OF PEOPLE MILLING about the lobby of Sunset Financial Tower. Normally, that would make her feel claustrophobic, but today it made her feel safer. She was still unsure about what had happened in the stairwell, but she couldn't help feeling like it had been purposeful—and personal.

One by one, firefighters filed into the lobby from the same stairwell she had come from, their tools slung over their shoulders. The crowd parted to let them through. Someone behind Veronica shouted, "Is it safe now? Can we go back up?"

A man toward the end of the train of firefighters, dressed in a black and reflective green uniform like all the others, looked up and nodded. "It stinks to high heaven in there," he said loudly, jerking his thumb toward the stairway door. "But it didn't spread beyond the stairs. Take the elevators if you can. If you can't wait for an elevator, I'd suggest holding your breath on the stairs." He laughed, as did the other firefighters within earshot.

Veronica wasn't about to take the stairs again. Not just because she was nervous, but also because she worked on the fifteenth floor. She was in good shape from surfing, but that was a lot of stairs. She eyed the lines forming at the elevators and weighed her options.

A hand pressed on her shoulder, and Veronica jumped.

"A little anxious, are we?" Craig Truman said with a sneer. "You know there's nothing to worry about, right? Some jackass tried to burn a file box on the stairs. Why not use a shredder, I don't know." He shrugged, as if Veronica had been the one to ask the question.

"I need to talk to you," Veronica said, her hand over her heart. She was still breathing fast. "Something happened down in the server room." She hitched up the strap of her toolkit higher on her shoulder.

Craig frowned. "Now?"

"You going somewhere?" Veronica nodded toward the lines of people waiting for the elevators. "It's important. Possibly a security situation."

Craig looked around until he locked eyes with Travis Payne on the other side of the information desk. He jerked his head, indicating he wanted Travis to come over.

Travis was short, balding, and beady eyed, and though he was only in his mid-forties, he looked ten years older. He had a slimy energy about him that Veronica had cringed away from since he was hired to replace Richard Newman as CTO six months ago. He squinted his black eyes in their direction, and Veronica fought down a shiver when he walked toward them.

As Travis approached, Craig pointed at a nook of empty couches in the far corner of the lobby. "Veronica has something to share," he said to Travis as he approached. "Let's find a quiet place for a meeting."

The lobby crowd parted for the CEO and the CTO, as it had for the firefighters—but to Veronica, it didn't feel like a sign of respect. It felt like they shied away from the men out of fear.

Information security was still a male-dominated field, and at all three companies she'd worked for since she graduated from college almost ten years ago, Veronica was the only female in the entire IT department. She'd had to learn how to stand tall and hold her own with men from day one, and it hadn't been easy. On the one hand, she understood why the people in the lobby were trying to stay out of Craig and Travis's way. On the other, it made her furious.

The two men sat on a long gray couch, far enough apart that they could sit wide-legged and not touch. Veronica sat across from them in a matching gray armchair. Perched on the edge of the seat, she leaned forward and spoke in a harsh whisper. "I found something odd in one of the servers."

The two men exchanged a glance.

"What were you doing in the server room?" Travis asked gruffly.

"Literally my job, Travis." Veronica fought the urge to roll her eyes at the slimy CTO.

Craig nudged Travis with his foot. "What do you mean, you found something 'odd'?" Craig asked. He tugged at the cuffs of his starched blue shirt.

"There was a...well, it looked like a chip, but I haven't had a moment to examine it closely. A chip where there shouldn't have been one, on one of the hard drives." Veronica looked around nervously. She didn't like having this meeting out in the open—but being behind closed doors with these two probably wouldn't feel much better.

Travis cleared his throat. "Did you bring it with you? Can I see it?"

Veronica hesitated. She had the hard drive in her toolkit, right there on the seat next to her. It would be easy enough to pull it out and show the man what she had found. But something about their demeanor nagged at her instincts. She shook her head. "No, the fire alarm went off before I could pull the hard drive all the way out."

The three stared at each other for a breath before Veronica broke the silence. "And when I was going up the stairs during the fire alarm, someone shut off the lights and tried to push me down the stairs."

"Who would do..." Craig started.

"This is a serious accusation," Travis talked over him.

The men looked at each other. Craig nodded at Travis, whose beady eyes narrowed.

"This sounds like the plot of a thriller. Corporate sabotage, attempted murder..." Travis said. He stopped when he saw Veronica's expression.

All the blood drained out of Veronica's face. "I never said anything about sabotage or," she swallowed hard, "murder."

Craig tugged at his cuffs again. "Of course not. What Travis is trying to say, I'm sure, is that you're making a big deal about nothing."

"This isn't nothing. I found something. And I think someone tried to make sure I didn't make it back here to tell you about it." Veronica did her best to keep her emotions in check and her voice calm—but all she wanted to do was scream at these two nincompoops.

Craig snorted. "You sound crazy."

"You pay me to keep this company and its data safe. I'm not crazy, I'm telling you something is very wrong here. I think you need to bring in a forensic technician."

Travis rolled his eyes. "And how much will that little goose chase cost the company? Hmm? You're blowing this out of proportion."

"And you're gaslighting me," Veronica spat. "You both know I'm the best in the business. If you won't listen to me, I'll..." Veronica stopped herself. She could feel her temper flaring, and she knew she'd say something she couldn't take back.

"You'll what?" Craig baited her. "I don't like your tone, and I've never liked your attitude." He turned to Travis. "You have to make the call, here. She's in your department."

Travis didn't even look at Craig before finishing the CEO's

train of thought. "I think your time here is done. You can leave now, quietly, and I won't embarrass you by having security escort you out. We'll have your office packed up and a courier will deliver your belongings to you."

"You're firing me? I uncovered proof of sabotage and you're *firing* me?"

Travis and Craig exchanged another look. Craig spoke first. "A person's reputation is such a delicate thing, don't you think? It would be a shame if word got out that you were involved in shady business here at Sunset."

"But I..." Veronica stopped, thinking of the standing offer at Pacific Wealth Management. One phone call from one of these men could not just close that door for her, it could end her entire career.

The two men stood, and Veronica stared dumbly. *What just happened?* For the first time in a long time, she was at a loss for words. She stood slowly, holding tightly onto the strap of her toolkit as if it would save her. She was a tall woman, but with their wide stances and crossed arms, Craig and Travis loomed over her. Her chin began to quiver, and she ground her teeth. She wouldn't give them the satisfaction of seeing her cry.

Just as Veronica took her first step toward the front doors of Sunset Financial Tower, Travis said, "Wait. No. Isn't that Sunset property you've got there?" He pointed at the kit dangling from her shoulder.

Veronica looked down, then raised her chin defiantly at the men. "No. This is my own toolkit. I've got the receipts to prove it. If you try to take it off me, I'll make a scene so big, the cell phone videos will be on the evening news." She pointed at the still-large crowd in the lobby. *Travis may be able to fire me—but I won't let these jerks intimidate me.* She stood up straight, pulled her blazer smooth, then walked toward the glass doors like she owned the place.

SIX
VERONICA

"THAT IS *BONKERS*," CARA SAID, PUNCTUATING HER exclamation by slapping her thighs.

"Is that the professional educator's term for getting fired?" Veronica said with a wry smile. She sipped her white wine and sat back on her overstuffed couch. After the debacle at Sunset Financial Tower, she wasn't in the mood for a night on the town. Thankfully, Cara hadn't argued. Veronica had only known Cara for just over a year, but she had been a thoughtful and caring friend from day one.

Cara picked up her wine glass off the carved driftwood side table next to the couch, took a sip, and shook her head as she swallowed her wine. "No, that's a history teacher's term for 'your bosses are setting themselves up for a whistleblower complaint'."

Whistleblower. The word crashed over Veronica like a tidal wave. Warmth rose to her cheeks, and she looked at her wine accusingly. "I'm no whistleblower. I don't even know what I found. I haven't had a chance to look at it closely yet."

Cara slammed her glass down hard enough to make Veronica wince. "Wait. Are you saying you still have it?" Her brown eyes widened, turning from doe-like to a bit maniacal as they fixed on Veronica.

Veronica nodded slowly. "I didn't mean to take it. I wasn't thinking when I put it in my bag when the fire alarm went off—I guess I panicked a little and just shoved it in my kit. Then when Craig and Travis fired me, and I realized that I had proof that something fishy was going on, I just...kept it." In her mind, she went back over all that had happened that afternoon. She remembered finding the loose bezel and discovering the bug on the hard drive. She remembered being startled by the fire alarm, her hands shaking as she tried to gather her gear quickly to evacuate. And maybe not so unconsciously putting the offending hard drive in her tool bag. *Maybe my subconscious knew a crime was being committed, even if I didn't have all the facts yet.*

"This is perfect," Cara said. She grabbed Cara's shoulders frantically. "You have evidence. You can prove there was sabotage."

"Maybe," Veronica said. She chewed her lip and tucked a lock of saltwater-bleached blonde hair behind her ear. "Even if I can show that this chip, or whatever it is, was designed to do something nefarious—steal data, upload a virus—that still doesn't tell us who did it or why."

"The reaction Craig and Travis had to your discovery was so suspicious..."

"I agree. But they're not smart enough to sabotage IT infrastructure, much less to do it under *my* nose. There are only four people in the whole company who have keycard access to that server room—and Craig is not on that list."

"Who else has access?" Cara asked, back to sipping her wine. She rubbed at the rust-red lipstick mark on the lip of the glass.

Veronica pressed her lips together, thinking through the three other people with access and what their motives could be. "Travis is on the list, obviously. As CTO, he has access to *everything*. Also, my application security lead, Dennis, and my IT infrastructure manager, Peter." Veronica frowned. "Dennis and Peter are both smart enough to plant a bug in a server. But neither would risk their job to do it. Dennis has a baby on the way, and Peter is here on a work visa. Travis may have access, but he's never been a technician. He doesn't have the know-how to mess with a server and not bring down the whole system while he was at it."

Cara raised her glass. "So Craig and Travis are the masterminds, but they didn't do the dirty work."

This wasn't a one-man hack job. The realization made Veronica's head spin. When she got into information security, she thought her primary job was going to be keeping data safe. Preventing hackers from getting into the data, and preventing malicious employees from taking out the data. She was no detective. At best, she was an overzealous data security guard. She stared out the bay window across from where she sat. The city lights glistened and throbbed like temperamental stars. It reminded her of the dance of lights in the server room. "Something isn't adding up."

"Well, the good news is we don't have to figure it out tonight. There'll be no one in the OSHA office to take your whistleblower complaint until Monday." Cara tilted her head back to swig the last of her wine, and her loose curls bobbed. The clink of the empty wine glass on the table echoed in the sparsely furnished apartment. Cara yawned and stretched. "Call me old, but I'm going to call it a night."

"It's only ten o'clock!" Veronica said, waving her hand at the clock on the smart-home hub next to her.

Cara shrugged. "This is why I'm a social drinker. At the end of a long week teaching a bunch of spoiled high-school kids, one glass of wine puts me out like a light—unless I'm at a bar flirting with handsome men."

Veronica cracked a smile at that. She'd often wondered how Cara could manage to teach history to teenagers all week and not just want to crawl into bed and stay there all weekend. Cara was upbeat and boisterous, balancing Veronica's more laid-back and logical personality. Cara was also an indisputable extrovert, while Veronica leaned much more toward the introvert end of the social spectrum.

"What are you smiling at?" Cara nudged Veronica's knee with the tip of a purple acrylic nail.

Veronica's smile widened. "Us. I'm smiling at us. Who would have thought a year ago that we'd be here on this couch together today."

"Indeed. You were so bossy." Cara cackled.

"Bossy! I was trying to save that man's life!"

"But I'm the one who knew CPR, bossy pants."

Veronica rolled her eyes. "I know, I know. I remember." She could still feel the dead weight of the drowned man in her arms as she pulled him from the waves onto Linda Mar Beach. She'd been surfing the north end when she saw the man fall off his board and not come back up. By the time she got to him and pulled him ashore, the current had taken them halfway down the strand toward a group of women taking surfing lessons on the south end. Cara had seen Veronica drag the man ashore, and she all but shoved Veronica aside when she reached them.

"Move out of my way!" Veronica had yelled at the curly-haired interloper.

"Give me room!" Cara had demanded, kneeling down next to the drowned man. She pointed up the beach. "Go call 911." When Veronica didn't respond, Cara firmly and calmly stated, "I know CPR. Go call 911."

Cara had begun chest compressions, but Veronica had stood there, not wanting to leave the man's side to go get her phone.

"Dammit, someone give this woman a phone!" Cara had called out to the gawking students of the surfing class.

When someone had pressed a cell phone into Veronica's hand,

she had acted without hesitation. She had told the 911 dispatcher exactly where to find them, and described with perfect clarity what had happened on the water and what was happening in that moment. Her whole life, Veronica had just needed something to *do*. She had never functioned well as a bystander. And here was this heroic woman with dirty-blonde curls taking over.

Now, over a year later, that heroic woman was the first person Veronica had wanted to call when she got fired. And once again, Cara seemed to have utter confidence in what to do—while Veronica spun, trying to find the *right* thing to do.

"Go get some sleep," Veronica said gently to her fading friend. "I'll take a look at the hard drive tomorrow and let you know if I figure anything out."

"Deal," Cara said, putting the back of her hand against her mouth to stifle another yawn. She stood and stretched.

Veronica walked her to the door and opened it. "Don't let the bed bugs bite."

Cara yawned again as she walked through the door and out into the hallway that led to the stairs and the stained-glass front door of the converted Victorian house. "Speaking of bugs, don't let the one on that hard drive keep you up all night. Mmkay?" She hugged Veronica tight. "We need that brilliant brain of yours on the case in the morning." Waving over her shoulder, Cara disappeared down the stairs.

THE WEIGHT OF THE DAY SANK INTO VERONICA'S BONES a few minutes after she locked the door behind Cara. She used what little energy she had left to brush her teeth, slip into short flannel pajamas, and pull the covers down. It was one of the few times she felt grateful for how tiny her apartment was—she only had to take a few steps to get from the pedestal sink in her minuscule bathroom to her king-sized bed that almost filled the entire bedroom.

SLEEP WAS JUST BEGINNING TO WASH OVER HER WHEN she heard the sound of a door handle being jiggled. Veronica sat bolt upright, her ears straining to make sense of the noise. It wasn't immediately close, so it couldn't be her bedroom door. *The front door.* Her heart galloped in her chest.

Veronica threw off the covers and dropped down to the floor next to her bed. She felt around under the bed for the biometric lockbox where she kept her Glock 44. Sliding out the heavy steel box, she placed her thumb on the sensor and heard the mechanical whirring noise that indicated the box had unlocked. She opened the top, pulled out the pistol, and popped in the full clip by feel, just as she'd practiced a hundred times since she'd moved to San Francisco.

"I'm armed," she yelled as she approached her bedroom door with her gun pointed at the ground. She listened, but heard no more noises. With the Glock still in her right hand, she slowly opened the bedroom door with her left. She looked out into the deep gray dark of the hall, but saw nothing. She heard nothing. Her hand shaking, she reached out into the hall and flipped on the light. The light didn't reveal the intruder either.

Slowly, two hands on her Glock so she had control of it, Veronica padded barefoot into her living room. With her elbow, she flipped the light switch in the living room, and did the same in the kitchen. Everything was quiet and still in the night. *Maybe I was dreaming.*

Out of the corner of her eye, she noticed something odd on the floor just inside the front door. Walking closer, her heart raced as she recognized the shape. It was a muddy shoe print—the kind of well-treaded print made by construction boots. Veronica reached for the door handle and turned it. Unlocked, it turned easily. She stood on the threshold and poked her head out, looking up and down the dimly lit hallway of the converted house. There was no one there.

But a trail of muddy footprints led to and from her apartment door.

SEVEN

ANGUS

ANGUS STARED AT HIS PHONE, TRYING TO REGISTER both the caller and the time in his sleep haze. It took two rings for him to realize it was his sister, and she was calling him at 2 a.m. He clicked the answer button and frantically, if groggily, asked Cara what was wrong.

"It's Veronica," Cara said, breathless. "Someone broke into her apartment. And she's going to blow the whistle because of corporate sabotage and you need to get over there right now and keep her safe!"

"Take a breath, Cara. What's this about corporate sabotage?" Angus turned on the lamp on his nightstand and sat up so he was perched on the edge of his bed. He slid his feet into the wool-lined leather slippers he kept perfectly placed on the floor where he got out of bed every day, so he didn't have to search for footwear in the dark—or in an evacuation.

"Never mind that," Cara responded. "The police are just about to leave, and you have to get there *now*. She's not safe alone."

"Why isn't she safe?"

"Someone broke into her apartment. I just told you."

"You said the police were there."

"And they're leaving."

"You think the burglar will come back?"

"I don't think it was a burglar."

Angus's head was spinning. "Cara, it's the middle of the friggin' night." He pinched the bridge of his nose.

"Exactly. She'll be alone. At night. With someone after her."

"Who is after her?"

"Dammit, brother, she's not *safe*." Cara took a deep breath. "Look, I'm not going to be able to do much if the 'burglar,' as you put it, comes back. My taser stopped working when I dropped it in the sink last year, and I got kicked out of self-defense class when I kicked the pervy teacher in the crotch. Veronica needs a protector. You're the best protector I know."

Angus's mind flashed back to his senior year of high school. He nearly hadn't graduated on time after getting suspended for punching a sophomore in the face. The kid's nose would be crooked for the rest of his life. Angus still wished he'd broken more of the guy's bones after what he tried to pull with Cara under the bleachers.

"Fine," he said. He heard Cara's relieved sigh on the other end of the line. "Text me her address."

POLICE CARS WERE PULLING AWAY FROM THE CURB IN front of Veronica's apartment house when Angus arrived. He slid his 4Runner into one of the newly vacant parking spots on the steep street and put the parking brake on.

There was no buzzer on the front door of the house, so he tried the brass handle. It was unlocked, and he let himself in. The first door on his right had the number 1a on it, and Veronica's apartment was number 2b. *Must be upstairs.*

He trudged up the carpeted stairs, cringing at every creaking floorboard, and found 2b at the top. The sound of his knuckles rapping on the door echoed in the dim, high-ceilinged hallway. He heard a shuffling noise on the other side of the door.

"I have a gun," a woman's voice hissed on the other side of the door.

"Don't shoot," Angus said loudly enough she should be able to hear him through the door, but quietly enough he shouldn't wake any sleeping neighbors. "It's Angus. Cara's brother."

The clicking sound of the door being unlocked was the only response. The door opened an inch, and a sea-blue eye looked out at him.

"I told her not to send you," Veronica said, confirming for Angus that at least he had the right apartment and he wasn't just scaring an unwitting woman half to death in the middle of the night.

"Cara is a poor listener," Angus said.

The blue eye in the crack of the door crinkled up slightly. Without being able to see the rest of Veronica's face, Angus could only hope that the crinkle was due to a smile. His hope was dashed for a moment when the blue-eyed woman shut the door. He heard the sound of something sliding on a hard floor, then the door opened wide.

The woman standing on the other side wasn't what he expected. His sister's friends had always been just like his sister, soft and effervescent. Veronica Clark was taller than average, with a lean, athletic build. Her blonde hair was pulled back into a low ponytail—or maybe a braid, he couldn't tell just yet—and her blue eyes were like electric steel. While Cara exuded friendliness (and a little silliness), this woman exuded strength. And it was clear her strength had been tested that night. In her right hand, she held a black handgun pointed at the floor. Her left hand was curled into a fist.

"Come in," she said, not moving. Her body was taut as a wire.

Angus slid into her apartment, though she didn't leave him much room to move around the gun in her hand. He noticed an open box filled with books right behind the door. *That must have been what she moved out of the way.* He pointed at the door frame. "You should install a chain lock."

"Yep," Veronica said coolly. She closed the door behind her, then used her foot to slide the box of books back in front of it. When she turned to face him, her sleek blonde braid slipped over her shoulder. She shoved it back behind her like it was a misbehaving cat. "So how does this bodyguard thing work?"

"Bodyguard thing?" Angus tilted his head.

"That's why you're here, right? Cara sent you over to guard me." Veronica made a sour face as she said the last two words.

Angus took a deep breath. *Thanks a lot, Cara.* He pointed toward the living room. "Mind if we sit down? I'm just coming off a swing shift, it's the middle of the night, and I'm too exhausted to have this conversation standing in a stranger's entryway."

Veronica nodded and pointed at the couch. "Have a seat. I'll make tea."

"Non-caffeinated, please," Angus said.

"I'm not a monster," Veronica said.

Angus had to look back at her to see if she was joking or not. Veronica had a slight smile, and her blue eyes were crinkled up. *The steel woman has a sense of humor. Huh.* He settled into the overstuffed white couch that sat perpendicular to a large set of bay windows. From his seat, he could see Veronica duck into and out of what must be her bedroom, then begin to move around the kitchen. The small kitchen was open to the living room, with a tall counter separating the two spaces. It looked newly updated and not entirely finished.

"An open floor plan in a Nob Hill Victorian? Bold move," Angus said, shaking his head.

Veronica laughed, a hearty sound that warmed Angus's mood. "I like natural light, so a galley kitchen doesn't really do it for me. Anyway, I can't take credit for it—I don't own this place. It was like this when I moved in." She set down the two mugs she had pulled out of a cupboard, and pointed to a large section of patched plaster in the ceiling. "The owners assured me they'd get the contractor back to finish the job, but that was two years ago. I don't think he's coming back."

Angus smiled. "I know a guy who might be able to help."

"Thanks," Veronica said, turning on the burner under the yellow kettle on the stove. "But that's the least of my worries right now."

"Why don't you fill me in while the water is heating up," he said, leaning back and crossing his arms. "Cara told me someone broke in, but she is incoherent when she's upset."

Veronica walked around the narrow counter that separated the kitchen from the living room, and sat in a pale blue wingback chair across from the couch. She perched on the edge of the seat, like she was at the starting line of a race and just waiting for the gun to go off so she could take off running. Her hands clasped and unclasped nervously, and her shoulders rose and fell as she took a steadying breath.

"Someone picked the lock. The lock on the handle and the deadbolt," she said, taking another deep breath.

"They got the deadbolt open?" Angus frowned. "That takes some know-how, and some serious patience. They must have been determined."

Veronica nodded her head.

"Did they take anything?" he asked, leaning toward her.

"Not that I could see. There were footprints leading into the living room, and a few more that indicated they'd walked around this room a bit, but nothing was moved or missing."

"Cara mentioned something about sabotage..."

Veronica looked down at her clasped hands, and her braid slid over her shoulder. "It's probably just a coincidence."

The kettle whistled. Veronica jumped to her feet as if she'd been stung. She put her hand over her heart and walked quickly to the stove, her long, lean legs carrying her there in just a few strides.

As suddenly as the sound had risen, it quieted. She poured the boiling water into two waiting mugs, set the kettle on a back burner, and carried the steaming cups of tea to the living room. Angus studied her movement. Veronica moved fluidly, but she didn't have a dancer's grace or an athlete's muscle tension.

Veronica handed Angus his tea. She smelled like sunscreen with a hint of rose, and he instantly realized why she moved the way she did. *She surfs. Huh. I was not expecting that.* He watched her carefully as she moved back to the chair across from him. He was certain now. There was a distinct way surfers moved in the world—balanced, light on their feet, but strong.

Veronica angled her body in the wingback chair to look out the bay windows at the city lights. "I love this city, you know. I miss a lot of things about San Diego, but San Francisco is such a special place. It's like the past and the future are dancing together in this city." She sipped her tea as she stared out the window.

"You must be tired," Angus started. "I'll sleep on the couch so you have an extra set of eyes and ears tonight."

Veronica shook her head and gave him an almost sad smile. "I'm good at my job. I keep hackers out of people's personal business, and I protect my employers. I'm smart, and I don't scare easily."

Angus didn't know how to respond, but he'd seen enough victims of trauma to know that sometimes the best response is just to keep listening. He took a sip of his tea, then set his mug down on a coaster on the side table.

After a few moments of silence, he said, "You should go to bed. You'll be safe with me here."

Veronica nodded. "Cara is always talking about you. You're a hero to her." Her words slurred and her eyelids drooped. She set her mug down on the floor at her feet, appearing too tired to even reach across to the side table. "I didn't want her to call you. But I'm glad she did. I do feel safer having someone here with me."

Angus smiled softly. "Go to bed. I've got you."

Eight

Veronica

Angus's words were ringing in Veronica's ears when her head hit the pillow. All she knew about this man was what Cara had shared with her—that he's a bachelor married to his job as a captain of a local fire station, and he's stubbornly protective of her. But she already liked him. That surprised her. She grew up with two much older brothers who ignored or bossed her more than they protected her, and she ended up in a career dominated by men who thought they knew more than a woman possibly could. She didn't like being in a position of weakness where a man felt like he had to come rescue her. So she wasn't happy when Cara sent her brother to watch over her. But after only a little time in Angus's presence, she was glad Cara insisted. She did feel safer with him there—and most importantly, he didn't make her feel weak.

Veronica must have dozed off, because the next thing she knew, the clock's glaring red numbers read 5:02 a.m. and Angus was yelling from the direction of the living room. She bolted out of bed, adrenaline causing her to forget to grab the gun that she had stashed loose under her bed when Angus had arrived. She doubled back and grabbed the gun.

"I'm armed!" Veronica yelled as she slipped out of her bedroom, her Glock pointed at the floor.

"Stay back!" Angus growled. His voice was coming from the front door, now, but there wasn't enough light in the apartment to see him.

Veronica froze, her hands glued to the gun. It took all her willpower to keep her finger off the trigger as she'd been trained to do in her gun safety class. A shape moved in front of her, and she raised the Glock in that direction.

"It's me," Angus said calmly as he emerged from the shadows of the hallway.

Veronica lowered the gun. "What the hell, Angus?" The heat of fury rose up her neck and into her cheeks. "You scared me to death."

"Someone tried to break in."

Veronica bit back a gasp. "Again?"

"Again. I heard the lock rattling, then the box of books sliding. I yelled, and then I heard the sound of someone running away."

Veronica sank to the floor. "I don't think my heart can take any more of this. I'm going to have a heart attack. Or maybe an aneurism."

Angus sat on the floor next to her, his knee touching hers. He was still wearing the clothes he'd arrived in, and he smelled like soap and sandalwood. She realized she hadn't thought to offer him sweatpants and a fresh t-shirt to sleep in, though she probably didn't have anything his size anyway. He was only a few inches taller than her, but he was much sturdier built.

"Are you having an aneurism right now?" he asked with a smile. His brown eyes twinkled in the slowly rising light of dawn.

With a start, she realized she was staring at his broad shoulders. She shook her head violently. "I'm sorry. I'm just having a hard time wrapping my head around this. Who breaks into the same apartment twice in one night—after the police have already been here?"

"Someone very determined."

Veronica frowned.

"It's probably time for you to tell me the story about the sabotage."

VERONICA HELD THE HARD DRIVE IN HER HAND, turning it from side to side as if she'd just found a beautiful new seashell on the beach. *So much stress and anxiety from such a small object. Small...but maybe not insignificant.* She turned it over again in her hand, then blushed when she caught Angus staring at her.

"You're sure this is why someone tried to push you down the stairs at work, and tried to break in here twice tonight?" he asked, a small line forming between his thick eyebrows.

"No. Not at all. But it's an awfully big coincidence. Your sister isn't crazy for thinking I might be in danger because of what I found. I've heard stories in my line of work—foreign competitors bent on stealing secrets, etcetera."

Angus snorted. "Sounds like a spy novel."

"Yep. But it's very real," Veronica said, setting the hard drive down on the kitchen counter. She glanced at the clock on the microwave. It was almost 7 a.m. now. Hopping down from her perch on the stool at the counter, she walked around to the kitchen. "It's time for more coffee."

"Make this pot extra strength, and I'll love you forever," Angus said, propping his elbow on the counter and putting his chin on his fist.

Veronica felt an odd flutter in her tummy at that. "Extra strength it is." As she began to make the coffee, she considered what to do about the hard drive. She could hand it over to the police—but they probably wouldn't know what to do with it. She might even get in trouble for stealing company property. She could take a look at it herself with the equipment she had at home...but analyzing a hardware bug was outside her zone of expertise, and there was a chance she would accidentally destroy the evidence.

"What are you thinking about?" Angus asked.

Veronica was surprised he'd read her movements so well. She glanced over her shoulder at the muscular firefighter sitting at her kitchen counter. "I'm thinking about what to do with that hard drive."

"I think you should take it to the police."

"I'm as likely to be arrested for theft as they are likely to hire a technician to look at that bug." She bit her lip. "Actually, strike that. I'm much more likely to be arrested."

Angus sighed. "You're not wrong. You did steal company property. And SFPD is woefully understaffed and overstretched— not likely to bring in a technician without rock-solid evidence of a crime."

Veronica laughed and shook her head, and Angus squinted his eyes at her. "Sorry," she said. "I'm not laughing about understaffed police departments. I'm laughing because those jerks at Sunset probably thought they could scare me by breaking into my apartment—but they just made me determined to uncover the truth of what's going on there." She took a deep breath. "I'm going to find out what they're up to. They're not going to get away with running me out of there. Or trying to push me down the stairs, or breaking into my apartment—twice."

"You can't be sure they did either of those last two things," Angus said, cocking his head.

"The more I think about it, the more I think it can't all be coincidental."

"If you're right, this could be really dangerous," Angus said. He rested both forearms on the counter, and the movement caused the collar of his black t-shirt to slacken, revealing a peek of his muscled shoulder.

Veronica glanced away quickly and tried to refocus her

attention on locating two clean mugs in the cupboard. "If they're after me because they're trying to get this bug back, or trying to stop me from finding out what it is, the best way to put an end to it all is to solve the puzzle."

"I don't disagree. But I still don't like it," Angus said, his face softening.

"I think the best place to start is to take it to George Keene, a digital forensic analyst I know over in Sausalito. He'll be able to figure this out much faster than I will. And he's less likely to destroy the evidence in the process." Veronica poured two cups of coffee, then turned and handed one to Angus.

"Great. When do we leave?" he asked, blowing on the steaming beverage.

"I'll call him now, but you're not coming with me when I go." Veronica sipped her coffee and leaned on the edge of the sink.

"Yes I am."

"No, you're not. I appreciate you coming over last night. Really. I felt much safer with you here. But I don't need a babysitter to go with me to visit my friend."

"Don't think of it as babysitting. Think of it as keeping Cara from worrying. I mean, have you ever seen Cara worried and upset? It's not pretty."

Veronica stopped herself from smiling at that. "Cara literally started a fight with the security guard in my office building when I was late to lunch one day and he wouldn't let her up to check on me. I was just stuck in a meeting that had run long, and I couldn't answer her calls." She pursed her lips. "Still, no dice. I don't need you tagging along on this."

"You don't have a choice."

Veronica raised her eyebrows. "This isn't 1950. I have *all* the choice." She stood up straight and crossed her arms carefully so her coffee wouldn't spill.

"You don't get to do that." Angus put his mug down, sat back and crossed his arms too. "You don't get to tell me that you think your former employer may be trying to hurt you, and then tell me to go home and forget about it."

They stared at each other for several heartbeats. Veronica felt her ears get hot with indignation. She didn't want a man coming to her rescue. At the same time, she did feel safer with him near. Maybe it was his physical presence, with his tall, powerful build and well-muscled frame. Or maybe it was his calm demeanor. He wasn't at all shaken by his encounter with the burglar. But her pride ached at the thought of him guarding her.

"What are you going to do?" Veronica asked. "Handcuff yourself to me?" She raised one eyebrow at him.

"Nah. I'll do something worse," Angus said with a smile. "I'll call Cara and tell her you kicked me out and ran off alone. She'll have everyone in the city hunting you down in five minutes flat." He smirked and crossed his arms a little tighter so his biceps flexed.

Veronica pressed her lips together and looked at the floor. "Dammit." Just then, her cell phone began vibrating on the counter. She picked it up and turned it over, instantly recognizing the number she saw on the screen. The blood drained from her face and she swallowed hard. "It's Craig."

"Don't answer it," Angus hissed, reaching for the phone.

Veronica yanked the phone away before he could grab it, and in doing so, she hit the "end call" button. She looked at the screen, unsure if she should feel relieved at the accidental hang-up or annoyed that she didn't get a choice in the matter.

The phone chirped. "Voicemail," Veronica said in a near whisper. She clicked the voicemail icon on the screen and played the message on speaker.

"*I know you have it. It's Sunset property and you need to return it. Now.*" The voice was undeniably that of Sunset CEO, Craig Truman, but there was a sinister edge to it she'd never heard before.

The growing knot in Veronica's stomach was quickly reaching

jagged boulder proportions. She locked eyes with Angus. Her pride screamed at her to hold her ground, but her fear begged her to accept his help. She took a steadying breath.

"Fine. You can come with me," she said, ignoring the self-satisfied smirk on Angus's face. "But I'm driving."

NINE
ANGUS

TRAFFIC LEAVING THE CITY ON A SATURDAY WAS AS BAD as Monday morning commuter traffic in San Francisco, and it took twice as long as it should have to make it from Nob Hill through the Presidio. Veronica couldn't be swayed from driving, and they were now crossing the Golden Gate Bridge in her blue Tesla. The green hills of the Marin headlands were coming into view. The fog was already beginning to burn off, and the clouds were retreating out over the Pacific Ocean, leaving a beautifully sunny Bay Area day in their wake.

Kansas's "Carry on My Wayward Son" blared through the speakers, and Veronica drummed her hands on the steering wheel in time to the beat. In her white tank-top and jeans, she looked both radiant and tough as nails.

"I didn't take you for a classic rock fan," Angus said, looking at her out of the corner of his eye.

Veronica smiled indulgently. "Considering you never met me before last night, what kind of music did you think I'd like?"

Angus tilted his head and looked at her carefully. "The Beach Boys," he said, without hesitation.

Veronica burst out laughing. "The Beach Boys! Why?"

He couldn't help but laugh along with her—her laugh was wild and infectious. When he finally caught his breath, he responded, "Because you surf, obviously."

"Obviously. I surf, so I must listen to The Beach Boys." Veronica rolled her eyes. Then suddenly she squinted a bit, looking puzzled, but kept her eyes on the road. They were almost across the bridge. "Did Cara tell you that I surf?"

"She may have. I honestly don't remember," Angus said.

"Then how did you..."

"It's the way you move." Angus felt his cheeks go hot. He looked out his window at the giant bridge cables rushing by. He took a deep breath. "Also, you smell like sunscreen." It was quiet in the car except for the guitar wailing through the speakers. He screwed up his courage and looked back at Veronica.

She was smiling from ear to ear.

Moments later, they were exiting the highway onto the steep, curvy streets that dipped down off the highway onto the small, Marin County town of Sausalito. As they drove through the colorful downtown, Angus caught brief glimpses of deep blue water and white sails between the charming houses. He rolled down the window and breathed in the smells of saltwater, flowers, and coffee. The sound of seagulls crying punctuated the traffic noise.

Veronica turned the Tesla down a small side street that quickly began to climb up a steep hillside. The Tesla hugged the curves, and Veronica drove like she could navigate these roads in her sleep. Her eyes slid briefly from the road in front of her to the GPS map on the dashboard display. As they climbed the narrow road up a wooded hillside, Angus caught broader, more sweeping views of the bay. Rocky, shrub-covered islands rose from the water east of Sausalito. Sailboats glided gently on the waves around Angel Island and the tip of Belvedere Island. The pines, oaks, and eucalyptus trees suddenly blocked his line of sight, and his eyes wandered to the beautiful woman in the driver's seat.

"Tell me about George Keene," Angus prompted.

"On paper, he's a digital forensic technician," Veronica said, not taking her eyes off the winding road. "But he's more than that. He's a real genius. He's retired now, but when I met him three years ago, he was consulting for Sunset Financial and a few other high-powered Bay Area banks and financial management firms." Veronica took a deep breath and breathed out sharply. "He's the only person I'd trust with this hard drive."

"How do you know you can trust him?" Angus asked. He shifted in his seat to turn his body toward Veronica, and he noticed she was gripping the steering wheel hard.

"He's done some consulting for the police." Veronica pressed her lips together and took another deep breath. Her blonde hair was tied back in a loose, low bun, revealing the line of her neck. Angus's eyes followed the line down to where it met her delicate yet angular shoulder. She was beautiful in a way he had never experienced before—tall and blonde, but also wiry and severe. If most beautiful women were like flowers, she was like a cheetah.

"We're here," Veronica said, pulling up in front of a mailbox with a line of live oak trees behind it so thick, Angus couldn't see the house beyond. "I'm going to text Cara really quick, and let her know where we are." She unplugged her phone from her car and typed a message. Then, reaching behind her seat, she pulled out a black messenger bag before exiting the car.

Angus got out of the Tesla and followed Veronica down the sloped driveway. The small, coffee-colored house nearly disappeared among the manzanita bushes, live oaks, buckeyes, and occasional fir tree. Veronica walked confidently up the short set of stairs that led to a wooden porch, and pounded on the side of the screen door.

"George, it's Veronica. Open up," she said.

Instantly on alert, Angus touched her shoulder. "I thought you were friends with this guy."

Veronica looked at his hand, then met his eyes. "We *are* friends.

Which is why I know he gets wrapped up in his work and needs a jolt to come back to reality." She pounded on the door a second time.

After about fifteen seconds of silence, Angus heard the sound of feet walking heavily inside the house, getting closer to the door, then a metal scraping noise as the door was unlocked. When the wooden door finally creaked open, a diminutive man with thick magnifying goggles perched on his head stood on the other side of the screen door.

"Veronica!" the man said.

"George." Veronica nodded.

"You didn't call."

"You never answer."

A slow smile spread across George's wrinkled face, and he pushed the screen door open. "Get in here," he said, waving them in.

———

WHILE THE OUTSIDE OF GEORGE KEENE'S SAUSALITO home looked like a cottage in a fairy tale, the inside seemed more like a spaceship in a sci-fi novel. The floors were tiled in neutral-colored stone, and the walls were stark white and dotted with modern geometric paintings. The entire back wall of the small house was glass, and the commanding view of the bay stopped Angus in his tracks.

George took notice of Angus's slack jaw. "That view is why I bought this ridiculous place." He stared out the massive windows, hands on his hips, smiling at the sheer expanse of sky and water.

"I wouldn't call this place ridiculous," Angus countered. He saw Veronica move out of the corner of his eye. She stepped up to the glass, put her hands in the front pockets of her jeans, and sighed. Angus could see the yearning in her pose, as if she wanted to melt through the glass and be carried away on the wind to the water below.

"I was supposed to be surfing today," Veronica said in a small voice.

"So why climb the hills to get *here*?" George asked.

Veronica reached around her back to pull forward the messenger bag she had slung across her body. Opening the flap, she pulled out the hard drive and held it out to George. "This is why."

George stepped forward, slightly unsteady on his feet, and took the hard drive from her hands. Frowning, he turned it over in his hands until he saw the bug. His eyes widened. He pulled the magnifier glasses down and peered through them at the anomaly. Without a word, he walked away, taking the hard drive with him.

Angus took a step toward him, but Veronica put her hand on his arm and shook her head. "Let him go. He'll be back." She turned back to the bay. "Let's just enjoy the view while he works."

TEN
VERONICA

VERONICA LOVED THE VIEW FROM GEORGE'S PLACE, BUT while it was captivating, it also made her feel a bit sad. There was something bittersweet about being able to see so much water all at once, but not being close enough to touch it.

She ached for the water today. The serenity of the ocean had been calling her intensely this week, and she had been looking forward to spending the whole weekend surfing. The last thing she thought she'd be doing this weekend was uncovering corporate sabotage...or beginning to look for a new job.

Angus stood at the wall of windows with her, unmoving. "If I had a view like this, I might never leave my house."

Veronica turned her head to look at him. "What's your place like?"

"The opposite of this," he said, laughing. After a moment of silence, he continued. "I live in an apartment above a souvenir shop in Chinatown."

Veronica smiled. "That's not a bad location. Good food in that neighborhood. Great parades, too."

"I don't spend a lot of time there. I'm at the station most of the time. On my days off, I keep busy."

"Busy doing what?"

Angus rolled his shoulders back and down. "Look at that sailboat down there. It's hard to make out, but I think that's the Captain America shield on the sail." He pointed at one of the many boats on the water near Angel Island.

Veronica was surprised at the twisting feeling she felt in her chest when Angus brushed off her question. They didn't know each other. He had every right not to answer personal questions. Still...it hurt.

They stood there in silence for what felt like minutes. The buckeye tree on one side of the steep back yard swayed in the breeze. Angus finally spoke, "I'm sorry."

Veronica turned to look at him. "Sorry for what?"

Angus's large shoulders rose and fell in a small shrug. He was still looking at the water. The midmorning sun reflected off his dark hair, giving him a halo. "I'm not good at this."

Veronica wanted to pepper him with questions, but her instincts told her she'd get more information if she stayed quiet. She watched her new friend carefully as he stared at the sailboats and ferries below. He seemed unsure of himself, which conflicted with his physical presence and the confidence he'd had up until now.

Sure enough, the silence didn't last long. Angus continued, "I'm not good at being anything but a firefighter. I'm not a good son or brother. I'm not good at small talk with beautiful strangers." His eyes flitted to Veronica, then back out over the water.

"It's the water, you know," Veronica said, turning back to the window. "Watching the waves move across the surface, the boats floating by—it looks like everything is in motion, but it radiates stillness. For some people, it's confusing. Overwhelming, even. For some of us...For some of us it stirs our souls and lays us bare."

Angus turned to face her.

Veronica took a deep breath before continuing. "At work, and in the rest of my life, I feel like I'm putting on a show. I'm strong, I'm smart, I'm accomplished, I know what I'm after. And then I get out on my board, and I just bob in the water until the right wave comes along...and it all drops away. Who I am at my core—the woman I am when I'm not trying—is exposed. But no one sees it because I'm out there alone."

"Are you a surfer or a poet?" Angus said with a laugh. He took a deep breath. "I see what you mean, though. I don't feel overwhelmed here looking at the bay. I feel at peace. And I can't remember the last time I felt that."

"We all need a little peace in our lives," Veronica said, turning so she was face to face with Angus. His energy was unlike any other man she'd encountered in her life. Warm and soft, yet strong at the same time. "I learned to surf when my dad died. I was seventeen. The only place I didn't feel either out of control or like I was holding things together by sheer will was out on my board."

Angus nodded slowly. "I dedicated my life to becoming a fire chief when my dad nearly died fighting a fire in the Castro. He and his crew didn't have the right equipment when they went into the building, and they knew it." He swallowed. "But there were a couple kids trapped in there. So my dad and his guys went in anyway. They never should have been in that position. I swore I'd not just follow our family tradition and become a firefighter, but I'd climb high enough in the ranking that I could make sure every company had the equipment they needed to stay safe on the job."

Veronica smiled softly. "Sounds like we have something in common. Our dads pointed us where we needed to go."

The sound of someone clearing their throat behind her made Veronica jump. "George, you scared the hell out of me." She put her hand over her heart.

George's forehead was creased with worry. "Sorry, but I've got something even scarier for you." He held up the hard drive and pointed to the bug on it with what looked like elongated tweezers. "This little sucker isn't American."

Veronica frowned. "What do you mean *not American*?"

George looked to the left and right, as if he were checking to make sure no one was eavesdropping in his own home. "What country is the biggest economic competitor to the U.S.?"

"You can't be serious," Veronica said. She shook her head violently. "Espionage?"

"Tell me the whole story," George said. "From beginning to end. I think this is bigger than you realize."

VERONICA, GEORGE, AND ANGUS SAT AROUND THE large wooden table at the back of George's Sausalito home, sipping a fresh pot of green tea. The room was silent except for the purring of George's Siamese cat, which had curled up on the spare chair while they talked.

"I don't think a foreign competitor tried to push me down the stairs during the fire alarm," Veronica said, setting down the blue and white bone china teacup on its matching saucer. "To know I was down there, what I was doing, what I found—and then to act fast enough to catch me in the stairwell? No way someone slipped in from the outside for that. It had to have been someone who was already in the building."

"I agree," George said, his wrinkled hands clutching his teacup for dear life. "And the break-ins at your apartment happened that same night. If it were someone outside the company, they would need time to find out where you live."

"It could have been Craig. He called and demanded I bring back 'Sunset property.'" Veronica frowned. "But he looked cool as a cucumber after the fire—and I just don't think a man that foul could be that good an actor. It had to have been someone else in the building."

Angus stared at the table in front of him, his brow furrowed. "But if that's a foreign bug, and we're talking about espionage here, why would someone at Sunset want to hurt you? And why would those execs fire you? Seems to me they'd *want* to know a foreign company was stealing information."

"That is the question, now, isn't it," George said, sipping his tea. "No matter the reason, someone at Sunset wants this kept quiet. And it's clear they'll go to lengths to keep it so." He set his cup down and placed a weathered hand on Veronica's arm. "Do you still have access to your work email?"

"Let me check," Veronica answered, pulling out her phone. She navigated to the company's email app and logged in. "Yeah. They haven't disabled my account yet." She frowned. "That's disappointing. We have an IT protocol when someone leaves the company. Their user credentials are supposed to be revoked immediately."

George gave her a pitying smile. "They're clearly lost without you." He pointed at her phone. "Still, it's good news for us. You may need that access to get information. Meanwhile, I'm kicking you out of my house."

Veronica stared at her old friend. "You're kicking me out?"

George laughed, a raspy sound now that used to be smooth when Veronica first met him. *He has aged a decade in the last two years*, she realized.

"I'm not really kicking you out," George reassured her. "But I think you need to get out of town. I'll get this to the right people at the SFPD. You need to go—drop off Sunset's radar."

Veronica swallowed hard. Her mouth tasted like copper, and she realized she'd been biting her lip. "This is surreal," she said, her heart in her throat. "I just wanted to surf all weekend and forget about my work stress. That's all. Now I'm out of a job and running from...I don't even know who I'm running from." She fought the urge to scream and slam her fist on the table.

George squeezed her hand. "I'm sorry. I don't know what you're caught up in, exactly, but I don't like the looks of it. And I think you'd be safer out of the city."

Veronica nodded quietly, the lump still in her throat begging for the release of a good scream. "I'll head back home to San Diego. I'm sure one of my brothers will let me stay with them for a few days. But I need to call Cara before I just up and disappear. She'll freak out."

"They may be listening in on your phone calls by now," George said.

"I won't tell her where I'm going." Veronica felt her grip on her emotions slipping.

"But they may be tracking who you're calling. It's not safe." The urgency in George's voice betrayed his worry.

Angus interjected. "I'll call Cara from my phone and let her know what's going on." He pulled his phone out of his back pocket and waved it.

When Veronica met Angus's eyes, she was surprised to see the concern there. Sandwiched between the handsome firefighter and the elderly forensic technician, she suddenly felt stifled. The chair made a horrible scraping noise when she pushed back from the table. "I need some air," she said. She grabbed her bag off the floor then made a run for the front door.

Eleven
Angus

"Leave her be," George said, grabbing Angus's arm.

Angus shook him off and sprinted after Veronica.

As he wrenched open the heavy front door, he shouted Veronica's name. Barreling through the doorway onto the small porch, he nearly ran right over the very woman he'd been chasing.

"Geez, Angus, I'm right here!" Veronica said after jumping out of his way. "What, did you think I took off and left you here? I just needed some air, like I said." With her mouth agape and her hands on her hips, Veronica's exasperation was plain as day.

Angus's heart was racing. He leaned on the short wall that surrounded the porch and put his hands on his knees. "Actually, I did think you ditched me here, yes."

Veronica shook her head, her frown etching lines into her sun-kissed cheeks. "I realize you don't know me at all, but I can assure you I wouldn't abandon you here with George. He'd force you to play bridge with him and his cronies. I'm not that cruel." She sighed and her frown loosened. "I need to get home and pack." She stepped toward Angus and stopped, her face inches from his.

Angus could barely breathe. Her blue eyes were like a stormy sea, and she still smelled like sunscreen and roses.

"Excuse me," she whispered. She looked beyond him to the door, then met his gaze again.

He realized he was blocking her way. "Oh," he said, stepping to the side. His cheeks felt hot, and he looked out at the driveway, hoping Veronica didn't notice.

Veronica opened the door, shouted her thanks and goodbye to George, then slammed the door shut again. "Let's go," she said, pulling her keys out of her bag. Angus felt a jolt of electricity when her arm grazed his as she brushed past him and began her ascent back up the driveway toward her car.

"That's it? We're just leaving the hard drive here?" Angus said loudly enough for her to hear him across the yard.

Veronica stopped halfway up the driveway. She turned sharply and said, "I trust him. He'll know who to take it to, and what they should be looking for. I'm good with technology, but this hard drive is George's world, not mine." She took a deep breath and let it out with a sigh. "And he's right. I need to make myself scarce while this all shakes out."

Angus nodded, then slowly began to follow her to the car. None of this sat right with him, but while bugged hard drives might not be Veronica's world, *none* of this was his world. He had to trust that Veronica and George knew what they were doing.

When they were back on twisty Sausalito roads a minute later, heading toward San Francisco, he could still felt that electrical charge in his bones from when their arms had touched. He looked at the dazzling, sun-kissed blonde in the driver's seat and wondered if she had felt it too.

Veronica turned up the classic rock station as she navigated the streets of Sausalito. Aerosmith's "Walk This Way" filled the Tesla. Neither of them spoke as she guided the car onto the 101 going south toward the city.

As they flew through the toll plaza, Angus remembered driving south over the Golden Gate Bridge when he was a kid. He remembered the endless lines of cars waiting to pay cash at those toll booths. Everything was electronic now, and that made everything move faster.

Faster doesn't mean better, though. Angus's thoughts drifted as the music and the sound of the road under the tires lulled him.

Soon, Veronica drove into the Nob Hill neighborhood. She cleared her throat, snapping Angus out of his reverie. "I'll drop you at your car," she said.

Angus shook his head. "I'd feel better if I stayed with you until you were on the road to San Diego."

Veronica nodded, but didn't say anything in response.

The music quieted as a call rang through on the Tesla's bluetooth. "Unknown caller" appeared on the entertainment system screen, and Angus and Veronica shared a sideways glance. "Don't answer it," he said.

"I wouldn't answer it even if I wasn't being harassed by criminals," she retorted. "I always let it go to voicemail unless I recognize the caller." The phone rang four times before it went silent and the music came back up. A moment later, Veronica's phone made a chirping noise. She jerked her chin at the phone on the dash. "Hold it up so I can unlock it with my fingerprint, then play the voicemail," she said. With a quick sideways glance at Angus, she added, "Please."

He did as she asked. The music quieted again as a voice sounded over the speakers, *"Give us the hard drive or we'll have you arrested for sabotage."*

Veronica's lips pressed together and her eyes grew wide, but she stared straight ahead at the road.

"Do you recognize the voice?" Angus asked as he set the phone back in its cradle on the dash.

"No." Veronica slowed the car to pull into her driveway. She was silent as she parked the Tesla in a small garage on the side of the converted Victorian. She remained silent as they got out of the car and walked around to the front door of the house, and led Angus inside.

As he walked down the hallway and up the stairs to her apartment, he was surprised that the house was beginning to feel familiar. He even remembered which step had a squeak in it, and stepped to the side of it to avoid the noise.

As they approached Veronica's front door, he knew something was wrong. The door was cracked open two inches.

"Stay back," Angus said, pushing Veronica behind him on the landing. She kept quiet as he put his eye to the crack in the door. It looked like her apartment had been ransacked. He pushed the door open slowly and motioned for Veronica to stay put. He could tell by the heat of her body on his back that she wasn't listening to his direction. Arguing with her would only alert anyone who was still inside, so he took a deep breath and pressed on.

A quick sweep of the small apartment revealed that whoever had broken in was long gone. As Angus made his way back to the living room from the bedroom, he found Veronica sitting on the couch, cradling a photo album in her arms. There were photos scattered about her feet, and it looked like the front cover of the album was halfway torn off.

Her blue eyes were misty with fear when she looked up and met his gaze. "They know where my family lives," she whispered, holding out the photo album.

Angus took the album from Veronica's outstretched hands and sat next to her on the couch. He opened the torn cover and saw a picture of a sweet little beachside home. The address on the house was as plain as day.

"You can't go to San Diego," he said, stating what was clearly going through her mind. "They know exactly where you're going, and you might be putting your family in danger."

"I know." Veronica took the album back and set it on the side table. She crossed her arms and hugged herself. "I have to figure out somewhere else to go."

"You're going with me," Angus said, putting his hand on her shoulder.

She turned to him, her eyebrows drawn in confusion.

"My family has a cabin near Truckee. We'll go there until this blows over." Angus put his arm around Veronica, fully expecting her to pull away. Instead, she collapsed into him. He held her tight as she shook.

"I'm in no position to argue," she said finally, whispering into his shoulder. "But don't you have a job to get back to?"

"Swing shift," Angus said simply. "I have four days off before my next shift begins." He felt her nod against his shoulder. "Go pack. I'll call Cara and tell her where we're headed."

Veronica lifted her head. "Thank you," she whispered. Then suddenly her eyes grew wide, and she shook her head fiercely. "No, wait. Don't call her. You know Cara—she'll want to come with us. Or at least she'll come check on us. We'll be putting her in danger. And—" she blinked hard, "I want to make sure she has plausible deniability."

Angus swallowed. "You're right. You're absolutely right. Dammit. Why does my sister have to be such a busybody?"

Veronica smiled softly. "She's not a busybody. She cares. More than anyone else I've ever met." She looked like she was going to say something more, but stopped herself. Her eyes rested on Angus's hands, which were now on her knee.

"I'm sorry," he said, pulling his hands back.

"No, it's okay," she said, leaning in and grabbing one of his hands.

Her lips were inches from his, and he breathed in her scent. He couldn't stop himself, he put his free hand on her cheek. It was every bit as soft as it looked. They leaned in toward each other, and Angus closed his eyes as her lips brushed his. The kiss was gentle, but not hesitant. She wove her fingers in his hair and pulled him closer.

A knock at the door interrupted the moment. Angus groaned as he pulled away. When he looked up to see Veronica's face, he was momentarily mesmerized by the wildness in her eyes.

"Veronica Clark?" a man's voice boomed from the direction of the front door. "Police."

"Coming," Veronica said loudly. Her eyes changed from wild to worried in an instant. They stared at each other for a heartbeat. Then, stiffly, she rose from the couch and walked toward the door.

He wasn't sure if the pounding in his chest was nerves or residual excitement from the kiss. Either way, he followed Veronica to the door.

"ODD THAT YOU'D HAVE A SECOND BREAK-IN SO CLOSE to the first." the more mature looking of the two male officers noted. His black hair was streaked with silver, while his young partner didn't yet have a hint of gray in his equally black hair. The officers sat at the island that separated the kitchen from the living room, sipping coffee with heavy cream.

Angus and Veronica both leaned against the sink, arms crossed. He looked at her, and a silent agreement passed between them, the same as it had when the police had knocked on the door twenty minutes prior. They wouldn't mention that this was actually the *third* break-in since last night.

"The neighborhood has gone downhill since I moved in," Veronica said with a shrug.

"I understand you weren't here when it took place. You're lucky your neighbor across the street called us when they saw your apartment being looted. On the chance that one of the other tenants of the house saw something, we'll go door to door," the younger of the two officers said.

"Don't bother," Veronica said, shaking her head. Her blonde hair had come out of its bun, and she had removed the pins from it so it fell around her shoulders. "Mrs. Kirkpatrick next door is almost completely deaf. And when the neighbors downstairs are home—which is almost never, because they're both startup founders and pretty much live at their offices—they can't hear anything coming from up here. These Victorian houses are solidly built."

"Still," the young officer said, his thin lips turning down in disapproval. "Better safe than sorry."

Angus's mind spun. Did it matter if the officers started digging around? Would it put Veronica in more danger? He made a quick judgment call. "Have it your way," he said with a shrug. "Mrs. Kirkpatrick has a bad heart, though, so go easy. We alerted her to a mouse problem a few months ago, and she ended up in the cardiac ward." He surprised himself with how easily the lies rolled off his lips.

The two officers looked at each other. The older one spoke first. "We'll take it under advisement." He nodded at the younger, and they both stood. "Thank you for the coffee. We have to be on our way, but please don't hesitate to call if you think of anything that may help us in our investigation." He pulled a card out of his breast pocket and extended it to Veronica.

She took the card and gingerly turned it over in her hand. "Thank you, officer. I will."

"I'll walk you to the door," Angus said, gesturing that direction.

He led the way down the short hall to the front door, and the officers followed closely behind. Opening the door, he nodded at them as they passed through. He closed the door almost all the way, but kept it cracked so he could watch them. Sure enough, they passed right by the neighbor's door and headed down the stairs to the exit.

Angus closed the door quietly and breathed a heavy sigh of relief. He leaned with his back to the door and saw Veronica peering around the corner.

"Are they gone?" she asked in a hoarse whisper.

He nodded. "Gone. It feels really strange not to tell the police what's going on." As he joined Veronica in the living room and saw the strain in her eyes, his internal conflict quieted. He just wanted to soothe her worries and see her courageous spirit rise again.

"It feels *wrong*. But until George does his thing, I may be incriminating myself if I talk about what I found." Veronica's chest was heaving under her white tank top. "The only thing I'm sure about is that I can't go to San Diego, and I can't stay here."

Angus put his arm around her shoulders and felt her breath slow. He turned his face toward her and found himself aching to smell her sun-blonde hair. "Let's get to the cabin. Maybe some distance will calm your mind."

TWELVE
VERONICA

MORE THAN THREE HOURS LATER, VERONICA WAS IN front of the Miller family cabin near Truckee—and it wasn't anything like what she expected. For one, it was much more remote. They had to drive several miles down a long, bumpy dirt road to reach it. She was glad Angus had insisted they take his 4Runner instead of her Tesla.

The other thing that surprised her about the Miller cabin was its size. For such a remote location, she expected something rustic. Perhaps a one-room log cabin with no electricity. What appeared before her through the trees, however, was a two-story house with a gray stone facade and a large wraparound porch. Angus pulled the SUV up in front of the well-worn stone stairs leading to the front porch.

Veronica stepped out of the car and looked up at the "cabin." The double doors in front appeared to be heavy red oak, and the balusters around the front porch were thick wrought iron. To the right of the house was an oversized garage, with one side large enough to fit a small trailer inside. Back and to the left of the house was a barn with siding painted the same gray color as the stone on the house.

"This is...impressive," she said as Angus came around to where she stood. He had thrown on a red flannel shirt over his black t-shirt.

"Glad you approve," he said. Then he must have caught her staring, because he quickly added, "It's clean. I always carry a change of clothing in my car."

Veronica looked him up and down. "I do approve. It brings out your eyes." She looked into the toffee-colored depths of his eyes and found herself drowning in them.

He smiled impishly and jerked his chin at the house. "I meant I'm glad you approve of our little family project. The cabin."

Veronica pried her gaze away from his face and to the house. "Of course," she said brusquely. She steadied her breath before continuing. "Though this is anything but a cabin. How does a family of firefighters and teachers afford this mansion?"

Angus snorted. "Do you notice what it's made of?"

"Stone?"

"Yup. A lot more fire resistant than your typical twenty-first century building materials. Clearly firefighters built the place."

"*Built* it?"

Angus held his hands out, then opened and closed his large fists. "With our own hands. It's taken three generations—starting with my grandfather, who laid the foundation. I come up here during my four-day-off stretches and do what I can before I have to get back to the city for my next shift."

Veronica realized her mouth was agape, and snapped it closed. She considered Cara her closest friend, but the more she got to know Cara's brother, the more she realized how little she actually knew about Cara's family life. It made her feel disoriented...and a little bit betrayed.

"Something wrong?" Angus said as Veronica took slow steps up the stairs toward the front door.

Veronica ran her fingertips over the polished pine handrails.

When she reached the top step, she spun around and sat down. "Why didn't Cara tell me about this?"

Angus joined her on the stoop. He leaned his shoulder into hers and gave her a little nudge. "Probably because she doesn't come up here. She hasn't been here in years."

"Why not?"

Angus heaved a heavy sigh and stared out at the expanse of forest that surrounded the house. "It's...complicated. Our family is complicated."

"From the outside, you guys seem like the Cleavers." Veronica felt a wave of sadness wash over her, and she crossed her arms across her belly. "I've shared a lot with Cara in the year we've known each other. We bonded so quickly after what happened at Linda Mar Beach. She knows about my screwed up young adulthood, and how my mom had to go on public assistance after my dad died, and how guilty I felt when I left for college. Why wouldn't she share this with me?"

Angus leaned back, propping himself on the top step with his elbow, and angled his body toward Veronica. A light breeze blew past, and brought with it the soapy scent of him. She looked away, out to the darkening woods.

After a moment, Angus cleared his throat. "Cara and I are a couple of screwups, if you ask our parents. They're mad at me because I've never brought a woman to one of our family dinners. Though, to be fair, they'd accept a man as my date, too—just so long as I was 'growing up and settling down.' And Cara...well, you know Cara. She's a free spirit. She loves her job as much as I love mine, but she also loves to party. My parents used to drag her here when we were kids, and she hated every second of it. The isolation...being here was her version of torture."

Veronica looked around her. The light breeze stirred the tops of the pines, and with the exception of birdsong and the odd cricket, it was utterly quiet. "How could anyone think this was torture?"

A smile spread across Angus's face, softening the angles of him. "She's one of those weirdos they call an *extrovert*." He winked at her.

Veronica burst out laughing.

When her laughter finally died down, Angus waved his hand toward the house. "Shall we go in?" He held out his hand, and Veronica took it. They rose together and walked to the front door.

Angus unlocked the door and pushed it open. As Veronica stepped across the threshold, she entered another world. The foyer was tiled in stone, with thick wood posts the size of whole tree trunks that marked the edges of the room. To the left was a comfortably appointed living room with plush brocade couches facing a large fireplace with a stonework mantle. To the right was a hallway leading to a large dining room—and beyond that, as far as she could tell from where she stood, was the kitchen. Directly in front of her was a wide, curved staircase.

"Let's get you settled in, and then I'll give you a tour," Angus said, pointing toward the stairs. He took her suitcase from her and motioned for her to follow.

Veronica picked her jaw up off the floor and followed him up the stairs.

AFTER A BRIEF TOUR, VERONICA WAS ENAMORED WITH the house. Every inch of it was lovingly crafted and thoughtfully decorated, and it felt both impressive and familiar at the same time.

Veronica set her single suitcase down on the queen-size canopy bed in one of the guest rooms upstairs. The bed was draped in a blue and white quilt and adorned with matching needlepoint throw pillows. She looked around the room and admired the quaint folk-artistry of the decor. The tall dresser with antique brass pull handles was made of a dark wood that matched the canopy bed. A delicate lace doily perched on top of the dresser, and on top of that was a lamp with a blue shade and white tassels. The wallpaper was a repeating scene of ptarmigans dancing among bluebells. The only thing more "countryside chic" than the wallpaper was the braided throw rug on the floor.

"What do you think?" Angus's voice boomed from behind her, and Veronica jumped.

"I think you like to sneak up on me!" She leaned against the side of the tall bed, hand over her heart.

Angus smirked in the doorway, leaning against the frame with his arms crossed. His flannel shirt strained at the shoulders, and Veronica found her eyes drawn there. The late afternoon sun cast golden light through the crack between the gauzy white curtains, giving him an angelic glow. Just for a moment, while her heart settled back into its natural rhythm, she let herself indulge in the thought of touching those shoulders.

"So?" he asked, interrupting her fantasy.

She blinked, trying to remember what he'd asked her. "Oh. Uh, it's great. Very cute."

Angus laughed. "I'll be sure to tell my mom you think her taste is 'cute'."

"I mean, I like it! I'm sure I'll be very comfortable here." Veronica tucked a stray lock of hair behind her ear. "Thank you again for letting me stay."

A slow smile spread across Angus's face. "My pleasure." He stood straight and turned toward the hall—then he stopped suddenly and turned back. "You packed your gun, right?" He pointed at her suitcase.

"No," Veronica answered. "I don't have a concealed carry permit."

Angus frowned. "We could have kept it on the dash, in view. It would have been legal to transport it that way. I don't like leaving you alone here without a weapon."

"Leaving me alone? Where are you going?"

"I'm going to go out for a run before I start making dinner. Care to join me?"

It was her turn to laugh. "Absolutely not. I'm not a runner."

Angus's eyes slid down her body and lingered on her legs. "You sure?"

She felt a sudden lurch of excitement at his gaze and reluctantly shook her head. "I'm sure. These legs were made for swimming." She laughed. "Besides, I need to unpack."

Angus shrugged. "Suit yourself. I'll be back in a bit. Spaghetti okay for dinner?"

"Yes, thanks."

"Good. Because that's the only thing I'm sure we have the ingredients for in the kitchen right now." Angus winked at her, then disappeared down the hallway.

Veronica stood leaning against the bed for a few more breaths. The exterior of the cabin was striking. Intimidating, even. But the interior felt intimate. It was cozy and warm, and called to mind snuggling by a roaring fire. She was confused by the conflicting feelings of gentle comfort here in the Miller family cabin and the fear that drove her here. Other conflicting feelings were causing her confusion as well—feelings having to do with her best friend's brother.

Veronica closed her eyes and steadied her nerves. She was safe here. She was safe with Angus. As long as she didn't lose focus.

Opening her suitcase, she frowned at the contents. *Should I unpack? Will I be here long enough for that to matter? More importantly, did I pack my toothbrush?*

Veronica moved to the window and looked out over the backlit woods beyond the house. It was quiet here. Between the noise and bustle of San Francisco, and the roaring of the waves in the ocean where she spent the rest of her time, she couldn't remember the last time she experienced real quiet.

Pressing her forehead against the window, she sighed at the peaceful surroundings. She was grateful for the momentary safety the cabin offered, but being alone here was bringing her thoughts back to the situation she was in. Someone wanted the hard drive badly enough to break into her apartment, but she still didn't understand why. Despite the attraction she felt to Angus, she knew she was putting him in danger. She also knew their time here was just a temporary escape from reality. Guilt lodged in her throat like a stone. She had to keep her guard up and not get too attached, but being with Angus made her feel alive and hopeful.

Her stomach rumbled loudly, reminding her she hadn't eaten a proper meal since breakfast. Figuring Angus would be gone a while, she headed to the kitchen to start dinner.

THIRTEEN
ANGUS

ANGUS RAN ON THE FAMILIAR TRAIL BETWEEN THE cabin and the river, and breathed in the scent of wet earth and turning leaves. It felt good to stretch his legs. He rarely ran in San Francisco. The hills were too steep around his apartment and the station to make running outdoors enjoyable, and he preferred weight training to running on the treadmill. It felt like a luxury to do a trail run. Still, his heart wasn't completely in it.

The trail was soft underfoot, the cushioned earth giving way to his steps. He tried to relax his mind and get lost in the rhythm of putting one foot in front of the other, but his attention kept coming back to the kiss—and to the look on Veronica's face when they pulled apart. In the short time he'd known her, she had seemed cool and collected, but the sheer lust in her eyes when their kiss ended had been animalistic. He couldn't shake the memory of it.

In the three hours it took them to drive to the cabin, he hadn't seen any hint of that passion again, though he'd looked for it desperately. They shared funny stories about Cara, took turns yelling at traffic, and listened to classic rock as they drove—it was an enjoyable drive. But the look of raw, fierce desire in her eyes hadn't returned. Had he imagined it?

The crisp mountain air filled his lungs as he found his pace. The forest was alive with the early twilight sounds of chirping chickadees and squawking Steller's jays among the rustling leaves. The weakening sun shone tenderly through the trees, dappling the forest floor with light. A doe and her fawn darted across the trail ahead of him, their white tails flicking their surprise at his approach.

As Angus ran, the peace of the forest was interrupted only by the sound of his footsteps. Usually, he'd be grateful for this moment of solitude and tranquility, but his mind refused to settle. His thoughts kept coming back to Veronica.

What if they'd met under different circumstances? Did she kiss him only because she was feeling vulnerable? Or worse, only because he'd come to her rescue? If he'd met her at a bar, or at the beach, would she have given him a second glance? His thoughts continued to spiral, which left him feeling frustrated and angry. Running had always relaxed him. *What is wrong with me?*

Angus reached the intersection where the woodland trail met the riverside trail, and he turned around to head back toward the house. He noticed a smoke plume in the distance as he ran—but he was so lost in thought, it took him several minutes to realize that the smoke plume was coming from the direction of his family cabin.

He immediately picked up his pace. September was too early for someone to be kindling a fire in a fireplace, and no one in their right mind would have a fire outdoors with how dry it had been. The smoke was grayish white, not black, so it was likely that water had already been applied to the flames, and it was unlikely that a structure was burning. Guilt and fear warred within him. He swore between quickening breaths. *I never should have left Veronica alone. We came here to keep her safe, to get her out of harm's way, and I just left her alone.*

It had taken him thirty minutes to reach the river, but it took him half that time to get back to the house. As he rounded the last bend of the trail where it curved to run along the fence line of his family's property, he saw where the smoke was coming from.

A thin plume of grayish smoke rose from the kitchen window of the cabin. Angus jumped the fence and ran toward the front of the house, skidding a little on the loose gravel of the courtyard. Halfway up the front steps, he stopped cold. The front door stood wide open.

Angus's mind ran through all the options. There was a rifle inside the house, in a gun cabinet in the basement—but he wouldn't be able to reach that without first entering the house. The only weapon he had in his 4Runner was a pocket knife. It wasn't much, but it was something. He stepped quietly down the steps and over to the SUV. Cringing at the unavoidable noise, he opened the passenger side door, plucked the pocketknife from the glove compartment, and slipped it into the pocket of his sweatpants.

When he turned back to the house, he surveyed the situation more carefully. There were no other cars here, and he couldn't hear any sound coming from inside the house. His eyes slid to the left of the house and rested on the barn. Was his dad's ax still out there? *Dammit, I don't have time for this.* He ran quickly and silently up the front steps and toward the open front door of the house.

Angus hesitated in the doorway. He listened hard, but heard nothing. He leaned his head inside the door, but saw no sign that anyone was there. The smell of smoke was overwhelming, but the foyer was visually clear—which meant the fire had probably already been doused. Reaching into his pocket, he pulled out the knife and opened the blade as he stepped into the foyer.

The house was eerily silent. Angus inched his way toward the kitchen, avoiding the places where the hardwood floors always creaked. Just as he reached the archway that led to the dining room that connected to the kitchen, he heard Veronica gasp loudly.

Angus ran full out into the kitchen, holding the feeble pocketknife in front of him. The kitchen was filled with smoke, but it wasn't thick enough to obscure the scene. Veronica stood slumped over the sink, swearing loudly with the water running full force. The curtains above the sink were charred and soaking wet.

"What the hell is going on in here?" Angus demanded at full volume.

Veronica jumped, and water sprayed across the kitchen, splashing him in the face. When she spun around, he immediately noticed how pale her face was.

Angus tossed the knife on the small kitchen table and ran to Veronica's side. "Are you okay?" He reached around and shut off the water, then wrapped his arm around her shoulder. She was shaking and clutching her hand.

"I burned my hand," Veronica stuttered. "Why were you coming at me with a *knife*?"

"I wasn't coming at you with a knife—I thought you were in danger and it was the only weapon I could find quickly." Angus ran to the refrigerator and pulled open the freezer door. He felt around until he found the ice pack he remembered was there. Ice pack in hand, he guided Veronica to a chair at the kitchen table and opened up her hand to see the damage. "It looks like something boiling hot splattered the back of your hand. What happened?"

Veronica took a shaky breath before answering. "I thought I'd get dinner started while you were out running. I found ingredients for a casserole, so I put a pan on the stove to heat up while I got everything prepped. Next thing I know, there's a grease fire. I grabbed the pan and threw it in the sink—and the curtains above the sink caught on fire. So much smoke. I grabbed the sprayer and hosed down the curtains, then opened the window and the front door to try to get some air moving through." Veronica turned her hand over and winced. "I got splattered by the hot grease."

Angus's ears were ringing. He sat down hard in the chair next to Veronica, closed his eyes and ground his teeth. Anger rose from his solar plexus and sizzled in his brain. "I thought Sunset had gotten to you," he whispered with his eyes still closed.

"What?" Veronica started. "No, I'm fine. Everything's fine. Just a stupid accident..."

"I thought they'd gotten to you," Angus said, his voice booming in the smoky kitchen. He slammed his fist down on the table. "Do you have any idea how worried I was?"

"I'm sorry, I..."

"Sorry doesn't cut it."

When Angus finally looked at Veronica, he could see she was fighting back tears—and she was angry.

Veronica didn't say a word. She just got up from the table, holding the ice pack to her hand, and walked out of the kitchen.

Angus stared after her, afraid to say anything more, and equally afraid of what he'd do if he went after her.

Fourteen
Veronica

Veronica stood at the window of the guest room upstairs, looking out over the darkening woods. Anger and sadness washed over her in alternating waves. The feeling that eclipsed it all, though, was the feeling of being trapped. *I could call a ride share. Or steal Angus's car. But where would I go? I suppose I can get a hotel room just about anywhere.* Her train of thought came to a screeching halt there. She knew she didn't want to be alone right now—not with Sunset's goons after her. It wasn't safe to go to her family, it wasn't safe to call Cara, and now she was stuck here with a man who seemed infuriated by her.

She closed her eyes and imagined the sound of the ocean, and the rocking of the waves. She ached to get back out on her board. It was the one place she always felt calm and never felt like she had to control everything. The ocean didn't give her the choice to control things. You either learned how to move in tune with the ocean, or the ocean would keep showing you how powerless you were until you got the lesson.

Veronica's phone chirped from the nightstand next to the bed, indicating she had a voicemail. *Odd. I didn't hear it ring.* When she picked it up, she noticed the cellular signal was alternating between one bar and "offline." She hit the play button and put the phone to her ear.

It took several seconds for the phone to connect to the voicemail system on such an unstable connection, but the message finally played. "*Tell your little friend to stop sticking her nose where it doesn't belong.*"

The blood drained from Veronica's face and she felt woozy. She sat on the blue club chair in the corner near the dresser and took slow, deep breaths. She didn't recognize the voice in the message—in fact, it had an electronic twang to it that suggested the caller may have used a voice changer—but the threat in it was clear.

Standing up, she tucked her phone in her back pocket, grabbed her purse, and went to find Angus. Whether or not he liked her anymore, he needed to help her get Cara out of the line of fire. It still didn't feel safe calling Cara—but Sunset didn't know where Veronica was, as far as she knew, so it should be safe enough to drive back to the city. Then she could figure out how to warn Cara in person without making her location known.

Veronica went down to the kitchen, but Angus wasn't there. It smelled like smoke and burned oil, and the window over the sink was still propped open. She closed it quickly before scouting the rest of the main level. "Angus?" The only answer back was her voice echoing off the walls of the empty house.

Her phone rang, and she pulled it out of her back pocket. Cara's name flashed across the screen, and Veronica ached to answer it. She hit the end-call button to send it to voicemail, then tucked the phone back in her pocket.

Veronica ran back upstairs, taking the steps two at a time. She poked her head into every room, but there was still no sign of Angus. *Where did he disappear to?* She heard a chirp, pulled her phone out of her back pocket and saw a text message from Cara.

WHERE ARE YOU?

As Veronica read the message, another one popped up.

I CAN'T REACH MY BROTHER EITHER. YOU GUYS ARE SCARING ME. CALL ME.

She checked the time. It was already 6 p.m. *I need to get on the road—I need to get to Cara before she does something reckless.* "Angus!" Veronica yelled at full volume. Still no answer.

Well, if he doesn't like me now, he's about to really hate me. She made a beeline back to the kitchen where she remembered seeing Angus's keys next to his wallet on the counter.

Sure enough, the keys were still there. She grabbed them off the counter, not even slowing down as she ran for the front door.

Fifteen
Angus

"Irresponsible. Boneheaded!" Out in the garage, Angus threw scattered tools onto a dusty workbench. A wrench landed on top of the growing pile with a satisfying clang. He picked up the wrench and slammed it down a few more times. His heart continued to race after his encounter with Veronica in the smoky kitchen, and nothing he did could get it to calm down.

He routinely ran into burning buildings for his job, and he had never been that scared. There was something about this fierce, self-possessed woman that made him anxious. It was infuriating.

With an exasperated sigh, Angus walked over to the ATV in the back corner and pulled the half-fallen tarp back over it. It was obvious that his grandfather had been the last one here. The old man was industrious and capable, but he was getting forgetful. He'd often wander off in the middle of a project and forget to come back to it. When Angus had walked into the garage looking for a place to hide out while he fumed, he had to do a double take. At first, it looked like someone had broken in and trashed the place. The proximity of the scattered tools to the half-assembled engine hanging off the back of an old fishing boat solved the mystery. He remembered his dad telling him that his grandpa had found a "fishing project" at a storage unit sale near Sacramento.

Angus looked back at the sad old boat perched between a pair of lifts, and remembered a time when he, his dad, and Grandpa Joe would have worked on a project like that together. Over the years, their family had grown distant from one another. There were good reasons for it, he rationalized. Cara's free spirit got freer once she was out from under their parents' roof. Angus had given almost all of himself to his job—and what remained of his attention went to looking out for his little sister. His parents didn't know what to do with themselves when it became just the two of them at home, so they found new hobbies. These days, the only thing connecting them all was his mother's insistence on a weekly family dinner... and with the swing shift schedule Angus worked at the firehouse, he missed many of those dinners, too.

Looking back on the last ten years of his life, though, Angus had never felt like he was missing anything. Until now. He liked this connection he had with Veronica, but it was also stirring a sadness in him that he'd been burying in his work. To open himself up to another human being meant that he couldn't give his full attention to achieving his goal of becoming a fire chief. It had never seemed worth it. But there was something about being with Veronica—being focused on her, and not himself and his goals these last couple of days—that had felt *right*.

The sound of an engine firing up snapped him to attention. *That sounds like my 4Runner*, he thought wildly as he ran for the door. Twilight in the Northern California woods was particularly dark, with large trees blocking out what remained of the light in the sky. But he didn't need light to see just where to go, because the headlights of his SUV were a beacon. Whoever was driving was in a hurry. The wheels skidded on the gravel as the 4Runner turned sharply and away from the house on the long dirt road.

Angus's mind spun. Should he run into the house and see if Veronica was still there, or should he follow the 4Runner? If she'd been kidnapped, there was no time to lose. If she was lying hurt in the house, chasing the SUV could cost her her life.

Watching the taillights disappear down the road, he made a judgment call. It was unlikely an attacker or a kidnapper would take his SUV. Chances were, it was Veronica driving away from the house in a hurry—which meant she was likely spooked by something.

Angus ran full-out back to the garage, nabbed a set of keys off the hook inside the door, and threw the large overhead door open. Running to the back of the garage, he tossed the tarp off the ATV as he slid to a stop. It took him three tries to find the right key on the keychain, and he didn't even give himself a split second to breathe a sigh of relief when the engine started right up. He peeled out of the garage as fast as the ATV would let him.

He knew he was losing Veronica quickly. He couldn't see the brake lights of the 4Runner as he drove down the dirt road, and the ATV couldn't drive as fast as the SUV could. Angus swore loudly as the silhouettes of trees whipped by.

The paved road loomed ahead, and he made a left turn, assuming Veronica was probably headed back to San Francisco. He rode the ATV on the side of the road, the left wheels on the asphalt and the right wheels on the shoulder. Angus was less worried about getting pulled over for driving a recreational vehicle on the street, and more worried about getting hit by another vehicle coming up from behind. This was a side road well off the main highway, and had little traffic, but better safe than sorry.

His worries for his own safety evaporated when he saw taillights up ahead. As he approached, he realized it was actually two sets of taillights—and one set was off the side of the road.

On instinct, Angus slowed his speed and shut off the headlights. He guided the ATV onto the shoulder, parked it, and slid off the seat. Quietly and quickly, he followed the light, praying he didn't trip in the deepening darkness.

Close to the two vehicles now, he was sure the one at an angle off the side of the road was his 4Runner. He couldn't make out the model or color of the other vehicle on the shoulder, but he could see it was a sedan of some kind—and the trunk was wide open.

Sliding behind a large tree trunk, Angus scoped the scene. The 4Runner didn't appear to be damaged. It had clearly been run off the road, but it hadn't hit anything that he could see.

He held his breath when he noticed movement, but the 4Runner was blocking him from getting a full view of the scene. Someone was walking around the vehicles, and it sounded like two sets of footsteps—but he couldn't make out who it was. Then, around the back of the 4Runner, two people emerged carrying something long and seemingly heavy. *They're carrying a body.*

Before he could think, Angus made a mad dash for the two people carrying the body. He let out a feral scream, and the people —men, he realized as he got closer—dropped the body. As Angus neared, they jumped into the running sedan without bothering to close the trunk, and floored it back onto the road. The tires squealed on the pavement as the car found purchase, and the brake lights disappeared in the distance just as Angus fell to his knees next to the body the men had dropped.

The only light he had to see with was coming from the SUV's brake lights, but the scent of sunscreen and roses was unmistakable. A loose burlap sack covered her head, and he gently lifted it to reveal Veronica's face. It was impossible to tell for sure in the low light, but it looked like she may have a broken nose. Angus swore under his breath.

"Veronica?" He put his hand gently on her cheek. "Veronica, it's Angus. I need you to wake up." Placing his hands on her shoulders, he shook her as carefully as he could. She still didn't respond. *Please don't hate me for this.* He gave her cheek a sharp slap, trying to hit only the soft flesh of her cheek and not bone, just in case she had other injuries besides the busted nose.

The slap did the trick. Veronica's eyes fluttered as she started to come to. She groaned and reached for her face. "Ow," she said. "What the hell happened?"

When Veronica's eyes met his, Angus was flooded with relief. "You tell me," he said, putting his hand under her head and cradling her on his lap. "You took off in my car, and I found a couple of guys trying to stuff you in a trunk."

A crease appeared between Veronica's brows as if she were struggling to remember. "I took your car..." She gasped. "Cara! We need to get to Cara. Ow," she said, clutching her head.

Angus's heart began to pound in his chest. "Why? What happened to my sister?"

"Nothing yet," Veronica said between gasps of pain as she tried to sit up. "She's nosing around at Sunset. I got a threatening voicemail from someone telling me to make her stop. We need to get to her before she does something stupid."

"You mean stupid*er*," Angus hissed. He slammed the side of his fist into the 4Runner's bumper. "Damn it, Cara, why can't you leave well enough alone?" Squeezing his eyes shut, he took a steadying breath. When he opened his eyes, he saw the pained look on Veronica's face. "We need to get you to the hospital."

She reached up and touched her nose. "I'm fine," she said. "Just got a face full of airbag when the 4Runner hit the tree."

"So you did hit something. I couldn't tell from back there." He jerked his thumb back to where the ATV was parked down the road. "An airbag can pack a wicked punch. You probably broke your nose." Angus helped Veronica into a sitting position, and his arms felt suddenly empty. Every bone in his body wanted to pull her back down and make her rest—but he knew better than to try it.

"I've hit my nose harder with my own surfboard." Veronica laughed, then winced. "I'll be okay. I'll probably have some good swelling, though. No laughing if I look like Rudolph the Red-Nosed Reindeer in the morning."

"No promises," Angus said with a pinched smile. He looked

her over in the light of the SUV, and he didn't like what he saw. Her eyelids were half-mast, her nose was swelling fast, and her blonde hair was caked in what looked like blood. He prayed it wasn't blood. "I need to get you to an E.R."

Veronica shook her head slowly. "That's exactly what they'll expect. Besides, checking into an emergency room would put me in the system. I don't know what data these people have access to, but if they can manage to get past all the security at Sunset, I wouldn't put it past them to have a hacker on the payroll."

"Is that how they found you way out here?" Angus asked.

"I don't know," Veronica said with a shrug. "They came up behind me on the road. I feel like if they'd found the cabin, that's where they would have grabbed me. More likely they tracked my phone somehow. My cell signal was faint at the cabin, but it was probably much stronger once I drove out of the woods."

"So they were nearby, waiting for you to come back online. Makes sense. It's terrifying and it reminds me way too much of *The Terminator*, but it makes sense." Angus shook his head. "This all makes me nervous. Let's see if the 4Runner is drivable and get you back to the house."

Sixteen
Veronica

Veronica cupped her hands over her eyes and leaned against the 4Runner while Angus assessed the damage. She groaned inwardly. *I'm definitely going to look like Rudolph in the morning.* The car sputtered as Angus tried to get the engine to turn over, but it sounded like a lost cause to her.

She barely came to the end of that thought train when the SUV roared to life.

"Yes!" Angus whooped from the driver's seat.

Veronica walked around and looked into the rolled-down window. "Is she seaworthy?"

Angus laughed. "The 4Runner's not pretty, but it should get us back to the cabin."

"And what about getting back to San Francisco?"

"That would require a miracle."

"We have to warn Cara..." Veronica stood up quickly, and pain lanced through her face. Clutching her nose, she squeezed her eyes shut tight against the stabbing pain. She heard the driver's side door creak open, then slam closed. Then she felt Angus's arm around her shoulders. His warmth sent waves of calm through her body, and the pain in her face was suddenly not so bad.

"Yes, we have to warn Cara. But we don't have a vehicle that will get us to her tonight. We have to find another way to reach her."

Veronica thought for a moment. "Is there a truck stop anywhere near here?"

"Sure. There's one a few miles down Highway 80. Why?"

"We may be able to get a prepaid cell phone at a big enough truck stop. Sunset may be tracking my cell phone, and they may be listening in on my calls—but they'll have a much harder time pinpointing my location if we call from a burner phone."

Angus's eyes lit up. "I like the way you think."

Veronica smiled, even though it hurt her face. She loved the look of hope in Angus's eyes—especially in contrast to the way he looked at her when he yelled at her in the kitchen earlier that day. The memory surged and drowned her momentary joy. *He's happy we're going to help Cara. That's all. It doesn't mean he's happy with* me.

Angus guided Veronica around to the other side of the 4Runner and helped her into the passenger seat. "Give me a minute to hitch up the ATV. We'll have to tow it back to the cabin before we drive to the truck stop."

"Okay, but we have to call her before 10 p.m. She turns her ringer off when she goes to bed." Veronica shivered as Angus stretched the seatbelt across her body, and leaned over her to buckle it. His black hair was close enough to brush her cheek on it, and it took all her willpower not to give into that temptation.

Angus snorted. "That explains why she doesn't pick up when I call before noon on the weekend." Still leaning over her, he looked up at her face. His eyes softened. "She's going to be okay. I'll make sure of it." He smiled. "It's what I do."

As Angus fetched the ATV and hooked it up to the tow hitch on the back of the 4Runner, Veronica turned off the cellular and wifi connections her phone. She wasn't sure exactly how they were tracking her just yet, but that should eliminate any possibility they're tracking her through an app.

Several minutes later, they were back on the dirt road to the cabin. The woods on either side of the long driveway were eerily dark at night, the evergreens silhouetted and looming like stoic giants, and she was glad the drive felt much shorter this time. It was spooky driving in the pitch dark, and the silence in the cab made her feel even more on edge.

Angus pulled the SUV up in front of the garage and jumped out. Veronica watched him in the side-view mirror as he unhooked the ATV, but then he disappeared from view. After a few seconds, she craned her neck to see if she could spot him. He was nowhere in sight. Just when she was about to get out and go looking for him, the passenger side door opened.

"I thought you could use this," Angus said, holding out an ice pack.

"Thank you," Veronica said, taking the ice pack. She couldn't find the words to express how grateful she was at this small gesture, so she left it at that.

An impish grin spread across Angus's face. "Wouldn't want you to have to guide any sleighs on Christmas Eve." He closed the door before she could think of a retort.

VERONICA LOOKED OUT THE PASSENGER SIDE WINDOW as they drove down Highway 80. The headlights from oncoming traffic hurt her head too much to look out the front windshield, and her heart hurt too much to look in Angus's direction.

In the silence, she mentally rehearsed everything that had happened since they arrived at the cabin. *Where did I go wrong? Did I misread him from the start? Or was burning the kitchen curtains such an unforgivable mistake that he could go from liking me to hating me so quickly?*

Just when her self-flagellation was hitting critical mass, Angus cleared his throat. Veronica risked a glance in his direction.

"About what happened in the kitchen. You know, at the cabin." His Adam's apple bobbed as he swallowed. "I'm sorry. I overreacted."

Veronica nodded. She wasn't sure what to say, so she didn't say anything.

"I just..." Angus started. His hands gripped the steering wheel hard enough that his knuckles turned white. "You scared me."

"How did *I* scare *you*?" Veronica seethed, remembering the exchange. "My hand was burned, I was suffering from smoke inhalation, and you acted like I'd insulted your mother!"

"All I knew was that there was smoke billowing from my family cabin—and when I got there, the front door was wide open. And to make matters worse, when I found you in the kitchen, you were clearly injured."

"Thanks for the recap. That still doesn't explain why you yelled at me like that."

Angus squeezed the steering wheel tighter, then released his grip. "I'm a firefighter. I saw smoke. And I thought someone had hurt you. I wasn't thinking about how to spare your feelings—I was worried and reactive." He breathed in deep, then let out the breath through pursed lips. "I'm sorry."

The 4Runner slowed as Angus guided it into the well-lit parking lot of a large truck stop off the highway. He pulled into a parking spot up near the main building and shut off the engine.

Veronica listened to the tick-tick-tick of the engine cooling. She sat there in the tense quiet of the Sierra Nevada night, neither of them speaking, until she finally broke the silence. "I'm sorry too. I didn't mean to light your kitchen on fire." She reached across the cab and put her hand on his where he was still gripping the steering wheel.

Angus turned to look at her and finally noticed her teasing

smile. "I was more worried about you than the stupid kitchen." He flipped his hand over to hold hers.

Veronica's heart raced as Angus leaned across the console and kissed her deeply. The rush from her head to her toes was sudden and intense as she sank into his kiss. She put her hand behind his head and pulled him into her, ignoring the pain arcing across the bridge of her nose.

Angus grabbed her wrist and gently pulled her hand from his head. As she began to pull away, sensing he wanted to end the kiss, he put his hands on either side of her face and held her there. Their embrace lost its intensity as he kissed her more tenderly now. "I don't want to hurt you," he whispered as his soft lips pressed on hers.

Veronica ached as Angus pulled back. He kept his hands on her face, and they looked into each other's eyes in the fluorescent light of the truck stop. So close, she noticed little streaks of grease on his face. His expression seemed to her a mixture of desire and regret—like how she looked at the ocean after a day of surfing, wanting more but knowing it was time to go home. She wished she could stay there all night...but they had work to do.

She sighed. "We need to go." It was physically painful when his hands released her face—and not just because her nose was tender from hitting the airbag.

Angus sat back in the driver's seat and nodded glumly. "Yeah."

They both got out of the 4Runner and stepped up onto the sidewalk. As Veronica approached him, Angus grabbed her hand in his, and held it as they entered the store. Its strength and warmth felt reassuring, and she could feel her nerves calming.

The truck stop store was less like a convenience store and more like a warehouse. It was cavernous, with massive steel beams above at least a dozen rows of towering shelves. Veronica pointed to a sign above the center aisle. "Directory," she said, not letting go of Angus's hand as she made a beeline for it.

Quickly orienting herself, she noted the aisle number for

electronics, and pulled Angus across the store to aisle three. The shelves on either side of them as they entered the aisle were tall and overwhelmingly stuffed with batteries, flashlights, boom boxes, headphones and other travel necessities. The back of the aisle, however, opened out into a small showroom. The shelves there were shorter, and interspersed with tables covered in laptops, tablets, and cell phones. Her eyes landed on a display of prepaid cell phones. "There," she said, pointing.

"We should get a few. Just in case," Angus said, grabbing three burner phones off the rack.

Veronica pulled one of the plastic-packaged phones off the rack and held it hesitantly. "I don't have cash on me. And if they're tracking my calls, they may be tracking my credit card purchases, too."

"I've got you covered," Angus said, squeezing her hand.

She smiled at him, pleased that he wasn't acting awkward about paying for the phones—even though she was certainly feeling awkward about it. "Thanks. I'll pay you back."

"You can treat me to dinner when this is all over," he said with a glint in his eye.

Veronica's smile widened. "Deal."

SEVENTEEN
ANGUS

BACK AT THE CAR WITH BURNER PHONES IN HAND, Angus felt like things were finally looking up. They had a way to reach Cara securely, and he could keep Veronica safe because the bad guys still didn't know where they were staying. Best of all, Veronica seemed to be just as into him as he was into her.

They got back in the 4Runner and he turned on the engine so he could get the heat going. The temperature was dropping fast now that the sun had been down for a couple hours. He looked over at Veronica in the passenger seat and gave her a reassuring smile as she turned on one of the prepaid cell phones.

"Here goes nothing," she said, dialing what he assumed was Cara's number.

He could hear the muffled sound of the phone ringing on the other end of the line. After four rings, Veronica hung up. She turned to him with a worry line between her eyebrows. "She didn't pick up. Should I leave a message?"

"I don't see what choice we have," Angus said with a shrug. He tried not to let his worry show through. Veronica didn't need the added stress. But his sister always picked up the phone—even when she didn't recognize the number. It was one of her more annoying habits. He'd lost count of the times she'd interrupted their weekly family dinner to answer a call from a telemarketer. "It could be important!" she'd say innocently, just before she explained to the caller that she wasn't in the market for a small business loan. Angus's heart pounded as Veronica dialed the number again.

"Cara, it's me," Veronica said, leaving a voicemail message. "I'm okay. So is Angus. Stop looking for us—it's not safe. Please. I promise one of us will be in touch soon, and we'll tell you everything. For now, just act like everything is normal. All our lives may depend on it. Later, skater."

"*Later skater?*" Angus said when she hung up the phone. "What the heck does that mean?"

"It's a stupid inside joke," Veronica said with a halfhearted laugh. "When we first met, Cara was taking surfing lessons. She told me she didn't have enough time to get to the beach and practice, so I told her she should take up skateboarding. It would improve her balance and coordination, and you don't need a wetsuit to skateboard." Her smile spread until it was ear to ear. "She told me she didn't want to be one of those 'grody skater chicks'."

"So you started calling her 'skater'. Makes perfect sense," Angus said with a chuckle.

"Hey, I was one of those grody skater chicks when I was a teenager. I consider it a term of endearment." Veronica laughed. With a sigh, she looked at the burner phone in her hand. "I think we should check in with George."

"Good idea," Angus said. "I'm curious if he's been able to learn anything more about the bug."

Veronica looked up George's number on her offline cell phone, then dialed it on the burner phone. It went straight to voicemail. She looked nervously at Angus before hitting the redial button. This time, George answered.

"I've got you on speaker on a prepaid phone, George. I'm in the car with Angus."

"I'm so glad to hear your voice," George said in a rough whisper. "I was worried they got you."

"I've got a lot to fill you in on, old friend," Veronica said. "But you sound upset. What's going on?"

"I couldn't get the hard drive to my contact," he said, wheezing. "They followed me. I couldn't risk it."

"George..."

"Listen Veronica. This is bigger than we both thought. There are more people involved—high-powered people who were getting rich off this data leak, and who would kill to keep this quiet. We both have to disappear until we can figure out a safe way to get this hard drive to the authorities."

Angus glanced at Veronica, and he saw that her blue eyes were wide with fear. "I don't understand why you can't just drop it off at the front desk of any police station," he said.

George's voice sounded even rougher as he answered. "The average police officer couldn't make heads or tails out of this device. It needs to be looked at by a professional—and professionals are expensive. A police department has to have reasonable cause to get that kind of budget. You can't just walk in off the street and accuse a massive financial management firm of sabotage."

Angus frowned. "Didn't you used to work for the police? Wouldn't they take your word for it?"

"I was a consultant, yes. But I retired years ago, and I don't have the influence or the connections there anymore. That's where my contact was going to come in." George sighed heavily. "We're wasting time. Where are you right now?"

"We're near Truckee," Veronica said. "Stranded. Angus's car is barely drivable." She looked sideways at Angus. "I got run off the road. It's a whole story."

George swore. "Sounds like we both had unfortunate

adventures today. It'll take me about three hours to reach you. And that's if I don't have to shake these guys off my tail."

"I don't like you driving in the mountains at night," Veronica said, worry dripping from her words.

"No choice, my dear. I can't stay here—and you and I need to make a new plan."

"There's a truck stop near Soda Springs. Meet us there." Veronica's hands twisted in her lap.

As they said their goodbyes to George, Angus wished he could do more than wait and let the techies figure out their next move. He looked at Veronica's anxious face and her still-swollen nose—though her nose wasn't nearly as swollen as he would expect from hitting an airbag. "I'm going to go in and get you some fresh ice. I'll get us some coffee, too, since we're going to be here a while."

"Thanks," she said, smiling wanly. Her brows drew down, and she put her hand on Angus's arm, stopping him from getting out of the car. "You know...I keep thinking about how Craig and Travis acted after the fire in the stairwell. After I found the bug on the hard drive. I didn't know it at the time, but now I know they were clearly up to something. And I wonder—what's their motivation? What were they getting out of it, or what were they trying to achieve? If word got out that Sunset Financial was hacked, share prices would plummet, and the shareholders would revolt. Craig would be asked to step down, and Travis would be fired."

"Sounds like reason enough to cover their tracks," Angus said with a shrug. "But it still doesn't seem like enough reason to break into your place, or try to hurt you."

"That's what I'm getting at," Veronica said, shuddering. "George said this was bigger than we thought. And I don't believe Craig or Travis would dirty their hands, or have the guts to come after me this way. I wonder if they're bit players in a much bigger conspiracy."

Angus mulled over his next words carefully. "I have an idea. But it's risky."

Veronica squinted at him. "I'm listening."

"I have a friend who's a journalist for the San Francisco Chronicle. If you shared your story with him, and made all of this public, maybe they'd think it was too risky to come after you again. There would be too many eyes on you at that point. We'd have to be really careful about meeting up with him—we couldn't risk exposing your location, but..."

Veronica cut him off. "Blowing the whistle publicly like that would destroy my career." She swallowed hard. "I can't do that. I'd never get another information security job."

"Is that such a bad thing?"

Veronica recoiled, looking wounded. "Yes, that would be a very bad thing. I worked hard to get where I am, and to build my reputation. I put everything I had into going down this path for the last decade. To give it all up...I...I just couldn't." Her shoulders slumped. "Besides, what else could I do?"

"There are a lot of things you could do. Like, you could teach."

Veronica burst out laughing. "Trying to get me into teaching, huh? Cara would be proud." At the mention of Cara's name, her face fell. "I'm worried about her."

"Me, too." Angus said. *More than usual.*

BACK FROM FETCHING BAD TRUCK-STOP COFFEE, ANGUS opened the driver's side door to find Veronica lost in thought. He slid into the seat and stretched across the console to hand her the steaming Styrofoam cup.

"Thanks," she said, taking the cup from him. She breathed in the steam. "Smells good."

"Smells better than it tastes, I'm afraid." Angus reached into his jacket pocket and pulled out a handful of sugar packets and creamer singles. He piled them on the console. "I brought these out in case you need them."

Veronica took a tentative sip of her coffee. "Smart thinking," she said, grabbing a creamer.

Looking at her out of the corner of his eye, he noticed the careful way she opened the lid of the coffee and poured in the creamer. Every move was calculated and graceful—from how she put the lid face-down so the condensation wouldn't drip, to how she cracked the paper top of the creamer single just enough that it would pour without making the coffee splash up.

"Tell me more about how you and my sister got to be friends," Angus prodded as he sipped his over-sweetened coffee.

Veronica's smile crinkled her eyes. "You know the beach story, right?"

"Yeah."

"I was in bad shape before that. Lost. Work and surfing were all I cared about. They were safe. I wouldn't lose anyone, and I wouldn't get hurt." She sipped her coffee and grimaced. "Ick. Better, but not by much." She took another sip before continuing. "Cara and I shared a traumatic experience on the beach that day, saving a drowning man. I think we both had the sense that we would need to talk about it afterward. After the paramedics took the man away, we found each other in the crowd and exchanged numbers. Cara called me that night and invited me out for a drink."

Veronica stared out the front windshield, her gaze soft and unfocused. She tucked her hair behind her ear and shifted her attention to the coffee in her hand. "When I met up with her that night, I realized something. Playing it safe and keeping people at arm's length wasn't saving me from anything. I could have been the one who nearly drowned in the surf that day." She took a deep breath. "I can't tell you exactly what Cara's experience was—but I think she was having an existential epiphany of her own. We started hanging out a lot after that."

Angus thought for a moment how to best phrase the question he was dying to ask. "But you two are...different. Very different."

"That's why the friendship is easy," Veronica said with a shrug. "We balance each other. I weigh my options, she jumps in with both feet. I temper my expectations, she thinks positive. She dances with any handsome man who asks, I watch over her drink at the bar." She laughed. "I think the only way we're alike is that we can both be a little overconfident in our professional lives."

Angus snorted. "Overconfident. That's a fantastic way to put it. I'll never forget that time she wore a Civil War-era dress to school to illustrate something she was teaching. She called me and begged me to bring a change of clothes to the school, because she was sweltering in the outfit."

"I remember that!" Veronica's boisterous laugh filled the cab of the 4Runner. "I was in meetings all afternoon, so I didn't get her message until after she'd already called you. You have to give her credit, though. Those high school kids will probably never forget that lesson on the Civil War."

Angus nodded. "Indeed. Cara is memorable." He sipped his coffee and sighed. "I'm glad you two found each other."

EVEN WITH THE ENTERTAINMENT OF SWAPPING FUNNY stories about Cara, the caffeine from the coffee wore off much too quickly. A couple hours after they downed the bitter black sludge, both Angus and Veronica were asleep in the 4Runner in one of the overnight parking spots on the edge of the truck stop lot.

Angus was in and out of consciousness, unable to get comfortable in the driver's seat. His eyes flickered open and took in the vision cast before him in the moonlit cab. Veronica was curled up like a cat, her knees tucked up on the seat, and her head resting on a folded blanket he'd found in the trunk. She looked small, almost dainty in that position and in that light—a far cry from the strong, statuesque woman he was coming to know.

He thought back to their earlier conversation and wished again that Veronica would consider talking to his journalist friend. Going public with what she found might discourage them from pursuing her further. Sunset would immediately come under suspicion if anything happened to Veronica after the situation became public knowledge. At least, that's what he imagined. The reality was, he'd never been in a situation like this, or known anyone who had been. If this were a movie, he'd be flying stolen helicopters and climbing skyscrapers to get Veronica safely to a journalist who would share her story with the world. But this wasn't a movie. This was real life, and there was no telling if the Chronicle would even run the story—and if it did, there's no telling if the public would believe it. She could inadvertently be cast as the villain in all of this—and Sunset wouldn't have to lift a finger. Maybe Veronica was right to be skeptical.

Just as Angus's train of thought came to a sleepy end, and he began to drift back into unconsciousness, he heard Veronica shift in the passenger seat and emit a little groan. "Everything okay?" he whispered in the dark.

"Kink in my neck," she whispered back. She sat up and rubbed her neck.

"Let me," he said, reaching across and putting his hand on the back of her neck.

Veronica tilted her face down, closed her eyes, and let Angus massage her slender neck. "Thank you." Her voice was husky from exhaustion, and her neck was as tight as the steel cables that held up the Golden Gate Bridge.

As he rubbed Veronica's neck in the dark, the memory of their last kiss flooded his mind and he ached to put his mouth where his hand was. He wondered if her neck was as soft as her lips had been. Just as he began to move toward Veronica and answer that question, a car pulled up and parked next to the passenger side of his SUV. A split second later, Veronica's burner phone rang.

She looked at the screen. "I think it's George." Her head snapped up, and she looked out her window. For a moment, she sat there frozen, staring, as if she were trying to make sense of the scene. At the sound of a car door opening, she shouted, "George!" and bolted out of her seat.

"I wasn't sure that was you I parked next to, so I called." George's voice was slurred.

Angus raised his eyes to the ceiling. *What timing.* He slowly exited the driver's side door, and made his way around to George's car—but he picked up his pace when he heard Veronica gasp.

George was collapsing in Veronica's arms and she was struggling to keep him upright. "I've got him," Angus said, scooping his arms under George's armpits and lowering the old man gently down to the ground. Veronica's phone clattered to the ground next to them, a sudden sound in the otherwise quiet parking lot.

Angus sat back on his heels, and when he looked down, he noticed blood on his hands. He looked over at Veronica, who was staring wide-eyed at blood on her hands and shirt as well. Squinting in the dim light, he looked over George's prone and wheezing form to see if he could figure out where the blood was coming from. "Where are you hurt?" he asked.

George looked at Angus with a bewildered expression. "I don't know," he answered. He struggled to sit up.

"Don't move," Angus said, softly pressing his hand to the man's chest.

"They shot at me. I didn't think they hit me, but..." He squinted and pointed at Veronica. "You've got blood on you. And what happened to your nose?"

"We need to get you to the hospital," Angus said.

"Wait," George said. He felt around on the ground next to him, then held up Veronica's phone. "You'll need this." He pushed the phone toward Veronica, who numbly plucked it from George's outstretched hand.

Angus scooped up the old man as if he were a child, and jerked his chin at the back door of the 4Runner. "Open that please," he said to Veronica, who stared wide-eyed at George, seemingly in shock.

She shook her head and blinked wildly, then opened the door wide. "Is he going to be okay?"

"I don't know. There's not enough light here for me to examine him. We have to get him to a hospital—now. Can you map the drive on that burner phone?" Angus gently lifted George into the back seat, and laid him down across the bench. He picked up a coat off the floor, wadded it up, and wedged it under George's head.

"Yes, I can navigate," Veronica said, her voice stronger and more confident now. She jumped into the passenger seat and began swiping and tapping on the phone screen as Angus ran around to the driver's side.

Angus turned the key in the ignition, and nothing happened. *Come on, old gal. You can do it.* He turned the key again, and it sounded like the engine was trying to turn over, but it still didn't catch. Angus sent up a silent, fervent prayer. On the third try, the 4Runner started up. He exhaled a breath he hadn't realized he was holding. Turning to Veronica, he said quickly, "Tell me where to go. And pray we don't get pulled over on the way."

Eighteen
Veronica

Veronica's pulse raced as they drove the dark roads of the Sierra Nevada mountains toward the nearest hospital in Truckee. She trusted that Angus knew what he was doing—after all, handling emergencies was a firefighter's specialty. But she wondered if it would have been faster to call an ambulance. Of course, then she and Angus would have to answer a lot of questions...and they'd be exposed to the people who were after her. Was she putting George's life at risk to save her own? Just as she was about to tell Angus to pull over and call 911, George spoke from the back seat.

"Leave me at the entrance and go," he wheezed. The sound of his wet cough was louder than the roar of the damaged engine.

"I can't do that..." Veronica started, shaking her head.

"You have to. You can't let them win."

Angus cleared his throat. "George is right. You can't risk getting on Sunset's radar. The hospital staff will know what to do. He'll be in good hands."

"This feels wrong," Veronica said. She felt the sting of tears and fought them down. *Now is not the time to have a breakdown.*

Looking at the phone, she announced, "We'll be there in fifteen minutes. Just hold on, George."

George coughed. "I'm sorry," he said, his words slurred. "I tried to get the device to my contact, but I failed. I'm so sorry."

Now Veronica's tears were flowing freely. "Don't you dare. You put your life at risk for me. We'll find another way to figure this out. The only thing that matters right now is getting you to a hospital." She stared out the window, hoping neither of the men saw her crying. She did not need anyone to pat her on the head and tell her everything would be okay right now. The trees blocked the moonlight, and the world beyond the beams of the 4Runner's headlights was pitch black—but it didn't matter. Veronica was lost in her own swirling thoughts. "Take the exit for Highway 89," she said, still staring out her window.

The next fifteen minutes felt like an hour, but eventually Veronica heard the sound of a blinker ticking, and felt Angus guide the SUV onto an off-ramp. She took the phone out of the cup holder where she'd left it and opened it to the map. "Head north. Then go right on Donner Pass Road."

Without a word, Angus followed her driving directions, and soon he was pulling into the hospital parking lot.

George sat up gingerly in the back seat. He reached between the front seats and pointed through the windshield to a dark corner of the lot. "Park over there," he said.

"The emergency room is over there," Veronica said, pointing at the brightly lit entrance.

Angus drove in the direction George was pointing.

"Take him to the ER!" Veronica snapped.

Angus shook his head.

"I'll be okay," George said between coughs. "This is the best way, my dear. We have to keep you off the radar."

Veronica's lip began to tremble, and a wave of fury washed over her. "You've been shot, George," she nearly yelled. "You can't walk to a hospital emergency room."

"Yes, I can," he said, putting a hand on her shoulder. "Trust me. Drop me off, then go."

As Angus parked the car in an unlit spot, Veronica turned in her seat to face her friend. "This isn't right."

George reached inside his coat pocket and pulled out the hard drive.

Veronica hesitated when he held it out to her, looking at it as if it would bite her.

"It's safer with you," George said with a small smile. He nudged it toward her, and she finally took it from him. "And another thing," he said, reaching into his coat pocket on the other side and pulling out a set of keys, "my car is in better shape. Take it. You're less likely to get stranded."

"How will you get home?" Veronica asked.

"I'll take the bus, of course," he said with a shrug.

Veronica nodded numbly and took the keys.

Angus hopped out of the driver's side, walked around the car, and opened George's door. He held out his arm for George.

George bobbed his head at him, and carefully stepped out, holding Angus's arm for support.

Veronica got out of the car and pulled George into a gentle hug. "Be well, old friend."

George squeezed her tight, then held her at arm's length. "You both need to go before anyone sees you."

Reluctantly, Veronica got back in the car. She waved at George from the window as Angus got behind the wheel and pulled away.

VERONICA RESUMED HER BLANK STARE OUT THE passenger side window as they drove back toward the truck stop to retrieve George's car. Ghostly trees swished by and registered only blips on her awareness.

"Penny for your thoughts?" Angus said with a sideways glance in her direction.

Turning to face him, Veronica opened her mouth to speak, but no words came out. She broke down into sobs.

Angus slowed the car and pulled it over onto the shoulder. He shut off the engine, unbuckled, and reached across the middle console to pull Veronica to him. For a few minutes, she simply cried into his shoulder—and blessedly, he let her.

When her tears slowed, he finally spoke. "He'll be okay, you know."

"How do you know that?" Veronica asked hoarsely, her throat raw from crying. She swiped a stray tear off her face. "You didn't even look at his wound."

"First, he drove three hours to get to us, and he made it the whole way." Angus gently stroked her cheek. "Second, he was able to walk from the car to the hospital. Granted, it wasn't a far walk, but if he was on death's door, I don't think he would have been able to do that."

Veronica nodded silently, still huddled over the console, trying to get as close to Angus as she could. His presence was reassuring, and she needed all the reassurance she could get.

Angus squeezed her tight. "I want you to consider talking to my journalist friend."

"No way. This situation is already out of hand..."

"Exactly. It's out of hand. This is the only way to get ahead of Sunset—to make it dangerous for them to make any more moves."

"No."

"What about Cara?"

Veronica swallowed. "She's safer if I stay gone."

"You know that's not true. She'll keep poking and prodding to find you, to find out what happened to you, until she pokes a grizzly bear."

"Cara *is* the grizzly bear," Veronica laughed.

The crease of worry returned between Angus's dark eyebrows. "She won't be safe until you are."

Veronica sat back in the passenger seat. She squinted at the headlights of a passing car. "Without George being able to get the hard drive to his forensic expert, I don't have enough information. I don't know what I'd even tell your friend."

"You'd tell him what you've been through. You tell him your suspicions. And then you let him take the hard drive to his contacts."

Veronica looked sideways at Angus and frowned. "You trust him?"

"Absolutely."

"Well," Veronica sighed, "I guess this situation can't get much worse. Okay, fine. I'll talk to your friend. But if he doesn't believe me...I'm not going to try to convince him, I'm just out of there. Got it?"

Angus smiled. "Got it." He started the engine. This time, it only took two tries. "Let's go get George's car, then get back to the house, get cleaned up and get a little bit of sleep. We'll head back to San Francisco in the morning, and I'll call my friend on the way."

Veronica felt suddenly exhausted. She pressed both hands over her eyes. "The sleep part sounds great." *The rest of the plan, I'm not so sure.*

Nineteen
Angus

It was nearly 3 a.m. when they finally made it back to the cabin. Angus had convinced Veronica to take George's ancient Honda from the truck stop while he continued to drive the damaged 4Runner. He worried about the 4Runner dying on the drive—the sounds emanating from the engine were truly horrifying—and he knew the SUV better than she did. If it croaked mid-journey, he could handle it.

"Knock on my door if you wake up before I do," Angus said as he threw his keys on the kitchen counter. "Don't try to make yourself breakfast or anything." He winked at Veronica and she rolled her eyes. Her nose wasn't as swollen as it was a few hours ago. Angus was relieved that she didn't seem to have any major injuries from the car accident, and he found himself relaxing a little bit more—especially now that they were back safe at the cabin.

"I'm too tired to punch you in the arm," Veronica said, half slurring with fatigue. "Just imagine I'm punching you in the arm, mmkay?" She walked up to him where he stood near the sink and threw her arms around his neck. "Thank you. For everything." When she pulled out of the hug, her eyes were glistening. "And I'm sorry I've turned your life upside down."

"You're welcome," Angus said softly, inches from those soft lips but too tired to do anything more than talk. "But you haven't turned my life upside down. Handling emergency situations is kind of my thing, you know."

Veronica's lips stretched slowly, sleepily into a grin. "I'm not a house fire."

But you are *hot*, he thought as he touched her cheek. "Goodnight," he said.

Veronica placed a butterfly-soft kiss on his cheek. "Goodnight," she whispered as she walked out of the room.

Angus leaned against the sink, his head swirling. The adrenaline had long since worn off, and his body was collapsing with exhaustion. Veronica's sweet goodnight left him feeling nearly delirious. The roaring in his ears and the heaviness of his eyelids reminded him that not only did he desperately need sleep, he also needed to hydrate. He downed a glass of water before shutting off the kitchen lights, double-checking the lock on the front door, and heading upstairs to go to bed.

As he reached the landing at the top of the stairs, Angus noticed movement out of the corner of his eye in the dimly lit hallway. He tried to focus his tired eyes. Suddenly a door on the right opened, flooding the hallway with light. Veronica stepped out of the bathroom wearing a silk nightgown that showed every curve.

"Oh!" she said, putting her hand across her chest. "I'm sorry. I didn't bring a robe, and I..."

Angus scooped her up in his arms and kissed her as he carried her down the hall to his bedroom. She nipped his neck as they crossed the threshold. Sleep would wait.

***

ANGUS ROLLED OVER AND LOOKED AT THE CLOCK. THE red numbers screamed in his eyes. *How is it already past noon?*

When he rolled back over, the warmth of the slender, naked body next to him reminded him why he lost track of time. Veronica sighed when he put his hand on her bare shoulder.

Not wanting to wake her, Angus slipped out of bed and into a robe, then headed to the kitchen to make a pot of coffee.

The kitchen still smelled like smoke. He knew from experience that it took a long time, some serious elbow grease, and a fresh coat of paint to get rid of that smell. His parents were going to be furious.

While the coffee was brewing, he went to the foyer and dug his cell phone out of the backpack he'd left there. His phone carrier offered no cell signal at the cabin, so it was pointless to keep it on him or to even keep it turned on—but he hoped his journalist friend's phone number was still in the downloaded contact list. When he powered up the phone, he was relieved to find Jackson Diaz's phone number still saved there.

Angus went back to the kitchen and dialed the number from the landline phone.

After four rings, he was sure the call was going to go to voicemail—and he was surprised when a live voice answered. "Hello?"

"Jackson," Angus said. "It's Angus Miller."

"My man! How you been?"

"You don't wanna know. Hey—I know it's been a while, and it's crappy of me to be calling you out of the blue for a favor. But I need help."

"You saved my cat from certain death. Anything you need, if I can help, I will."

Angus felt a rush of relief. "Thanks, man. To be honest, the favor is for a...friend." It felt awkward to call Veronica a friend after the night they just shared. "She's in trouble. She found evidence of espionage and the company fired her. She took the evidence with her, and someone has been after her ever since. We're staying off the radar for now."

"Wow," Jackson said. "How can I help?"

"I want to make it hard for these guys to come after her. I think if she blew the whistle on this, made it public, it would be too risky for them to hurt her."

"I see. Are you at liberty to tell me what company she was working for?"

"I think I should let Veronica tell her own story. But I can tell you it's a big financial services company located in the Financial District."

There was silence on the line for a beat too long.

"You still there?" Angus prompted.

"Yeah," Jackson replied. "It's not Sunset Financial, is it?"

Angus swallowed. "What if it is?"

"Son-of-a-gun. If it is, you may be handing me a miracle. A colleague and I have been piecing together a story for the last six months that'll turn the Bay Area on its head. But we haven't been able to get access to anyone on the inside, and that's really what we need to make sense of the last piece of this puzzle. When can I talk to your friend? Did you say her name is Veronica?"

"Yeah, Veronica. I'll have her call you..."

"No. Angus, I need to talk to her in person. Can you arrange that?"

Angus thought of the sleeping woman upstairs in his bed, the delicate curve of her neck, and the sweet way she sighs in her sleep. "Let me talk to her. I'll call you back."

After the men said their goodbyes, Angus sat at the kitchen table and stared at the phone on the wall. George said this was more serious than we realized. Now Jackson seems to know something too. This all feels bigger than one woman can handle— even if that woman is whip smart and stronger than most firefighters I know.

As if his thoughts conjured her, Veronica walked into the kitchen wearing one of his white t-shirts knotted at the waist over a pair of skin-tight jeans. Her long, blonde hair was in a low braid down her back, and tiny wisps of escaped strands framed her cheekbones.

"Hope you don't mind that I borrowed this out of your drawer," she said, her voice still husky with fatigue. She motioned at the shirt. "Apparently I forgot to pack a clean shirt."

Angus snapped his gaping jaw shut and composed himself before he answered. "Of course. Perfectly okay." He cleared his throat, then waved at the coffee maker. "Coffee's made. Cups are in the upper cupboard to the right of the sink."

He watched Veronica as she perched on the balls of her feet and stretched her long, lean legs to raise herself high enough to reach the coffee cup she wanted on the second shelf. She pulled down the raku pottery mug and turned it over in her hand. "This is beautiful."

"I thought so, too, when I saw it. I bought that set from a local ceramic artist," Angus said.

"You have good taste," Veronica said with a smile.

Angus rose from his seat at the table and crossed the kitchen. He wrapped his arms around Veronica's waist and kissed her deeply. "I *do* have good taste," he said, teasing her lip with his teeth.

He sighed, lingering there with his forehead pressed against hers. He didn't want to stop kissing her...ever. But there was a pressing situation to talk about.

"I called my journalist friend, Jackson, this morning," Angus said.

Veronica leaned back and looked at him. "And?"

"And he wants to talk to you. In person." Angus lightly stroked her cheek with his thumb. "He thinks what you found may be related to a story he's already pursuing."

"Wait. What?" Veronica's eyes caught and held his, their seafoam and sapphire hues flashing in the sunlight streaming through one of the kitchen windows. "He's already doing a story on Sunset?"

"Sounds like it."

Veronica bit her lip as she contemplated this new information. "So I might not be on my own, here."

"You were never on your own," Angus said, tucking a stray lock of hair behind her ear. When she smiled at him, he felt warmth right down to his toes.

Veronica leaned in and kissed him softly, then passionately, pulling his body against hers. They were so wrapped up in each other, they both nearly jumped out of their skin when someone cleared their throat.

"Well, now I know why you haven't been picking up the phone," Cara said from the doorway. She had one hand on her ample hip and a wicked grin on her face.

"Cara!" Veronica said, nearly bowling Angus down as she ran to her friend and embraced her. "I'm so glad you're okay."

"Why wouldn't I be okay?" Cara said, still hugging Veronica. "And what the hell happened to your nose?"

"Long story," Veronica mumbled into Cara's hair.

When Veronica finally let go, Angus swooped in to take her place. He squeezed his sister tight and picked her up off the ground like he used to do when they were kids. "I've never been so happy to see my annoying little sister."

"Put me down!" Cara squealed. When he obeyed, she playfully punched him in the shoulder. "What is *up* with you two? Besides your new love of playing tonsil hockey, that is. I've been worried sick!"

"It's a long story," Veronica said.

"And you couldn't call me and tell me?"

Veronica and Angus exchanged a look. "No," Veronica said. "It was too dangerous."

"Well, fill me in," Cara said, throwing her bohemian purse on the counter. She flicked her chin at the coffee pot and her dirty-blonde curls bounced. "Is that fresh?"

Angus nodded.

"Great. I need caffeine after that drive." Cara grabbed a mug out of the cupboard. "Now, talk." While she poured a cup of coffee, she kept one eye on Angus and Veronica, as if she was afraid they'd bolt if she looked away.

"Wait," Angus said, his brows drawing down. "How did you know we were here?"

Cara rolled her eyes. "Where else would you go?"

Angus frowned. Was he that easy to predict?

Veronica poured a fresh cup of coffee and joined Cara and Angus at the table. Twenty minutes later, Cara was caught up on the last few days. At least, caught up on the events surrounding the hard drive.

"Is George okay?" Cara asked, her green eyes pinched with concern.

"I don't know," Veronica said with a sigh. "I tried calling him when I woke up this morning, but he didn't answer."

"And the hard drive?" Cara asked.

"It's upstairs," Veronica answered. "Angus's journalist friend may be able to help us get answers about it. That's the only hope I have right now."

Cara looked from Veronica to Angus and back again, then shook her head. "Well, my little lovebirds, then we know what we have to do." When she received only quizzical looks in response, she added, "Let's go! Let's get Veronica to the newsman. What was his name?"

"Jackson," Angus supplied.

"Let's get Veronica to Jackson. That sounds like a bad country song." She stood up from the table and clapped her hands twice. "Chop chop! Get your stuff. It's a long drive, and I have to teach a bunch of freshmen about the American Revolution tomorrow morning."

TWENTY
VERONICA

"So. You and my brother, huh?" Cara teased as she drove her gray Prius down the long dirt drive leading from the cabin to the main road.

Veronica snuck a look at her friend and was relieved to see nothing but amusement on her face. "Yeah. It just sort of...happened."

Cara's smile spread wide. "I'm only surprised it took this long for you two to meet. I knew you'd hit it off."

Veronica raised an eyebrow. "How do you figure? When he showed up at my apartment, I thought he had a savior complex. I wasn't thinking 'ooh, let's get it on'."

"His first impressions *are* pretty special." Cara laughed. "Seriously, though, you two are a lot alike. You're both total bosses —in the best way, of course. You're take-charge types who don't like to ask for help. And your hearts are made of solid gold."

Veronica thought back to the last few days. Angus did have a beautiful heart. Unfortunately, she didn't have a great track record with taking care of beautiful things. What if this didn't work out? What if she hurt him? It would hurt Cara, too. *What have I done?*

Cara glanced at the rearview mirror, no doubt making sure

Angus was still behind them in George's car. As if reading Veronica's thoughts, she added, "You're both good eggs. And you're both stubborn and too independent for your own good. I'm glad you have each other."

"Cara, I..." Veronica didn't really know what to say. She was falling for Angus—hard—and it scared her more than Sunset's goons did. "This is really new. I'm not sure what I have with Angus. Are you going to be okay if it turns out to be nothing?"

Cara snorted. "It's not nothing. I saw the way you looked at each other before you realized I was there." She sped up to get around a slow driver on the highway.

Veronica noticed Cara sneaking looks at her out of the corner of her eye. She frowned nervously.

"I'll be fine," Cara said with a sigh. "See, *this* is why you two are such a good match. You're both annoyingly overprotective."

The lump in Veronica's throat returned with a vengeance, and she shook her head. "You put yourself at risk nosing around Sunset, you know. It's hard to not feel protective when you're throwing yourself into the line of fire."

"I didn't nose around Sunset," Cara argued, frowning.

"They left me a voicemail warning me to tell you to stop 'sticking your nose where it doesn't belong.' What exactly were you doing?"

"Other than stopping by your apartment, I didn't do anything."

Veronica swallowed hard. "So they've got eyes on my apartment."

Cara was silent for longer than usual. When she finally spoke, she asked Veronica to hand her the cell phone she'd tucked into the console of her Prius. Cara unlocked the phone with her fingerprint. "Will you please call Angus? He's in my favorites list in the Contacts app."

Veronica obliged.

"Angus, it's your sister," Cara said into the air as Angus's hello boomed over the Bluetooth speaker in the ceiling of the car. "I think we need to take Veronica straight to your friend's place. I don't think it's safe for us to stop at her apartment first. Will you text me the address?"

"Sure," Angus said. "But why?"

"We think Sunset may have eyes on it," Cara answered with a sideways glance to Veronica.

Angus swore. "Okay. Let's stop at a gas station near Auburn. I'll text you when I'm pulled over."

Twenty-One
Angus

Since stopping in Auburn and making a plan to drop Veronica off at Jackson's apartment, Angus had felt unsettled. As he drove over the Bay Bridge and got his first glimpse of San Francisco in days, the constricting feeling in his chest only grew. He still believed that getting Veronica's story out to the public was the best way to keep Sunset at a distance—and he trusted Jackson. But knowing that Veronica's apartment was being watched, and that Cara was in Sunset's crosshairs too...it made him nervous.

The city was backlit by the descending late-afternoon sun, giving it a stone-like veneer. It felt less like Angus was driving into the vibrant, dramatic city he called home, and more like he was driving into a mausoleum. He rolled down his window and let the cool, moist air of the bay caress his skin.

Angus prided himself on having a cool head in all circumstances. He didn't *get* nervous. No matter how stressful the situation, no matter how dire the circumstances, he kept a cool head—because in his line of work, his state of mind was a matter of life and death.

He remembered back to one of the first fires he was ever called to. An apartment had gone up in flames, and the fire was spreading fast. A structure fire in an urban area was one of the most difficult circumstances to navigate, especially in heavy gear. With a helmet and respirator, he had little peripheral vision. Hauling the hose line was difficult in tight spaces. And modern furnishings burn hot and fast, and produce thick black smoke. At one point during the blaze, Angus got turned around and lost his crew. Two men were supposed to be on the hose line, but as far as he could tell through the smoke, he was on his own. While his heart raced with fear, his mind had become astonishingly clear. He recalled his training, and began feeling along the hose line, following it through the building. Just as he passed from the apartment into the hall, the ceiling in the apartment collapsed with a deafening sound.

His crew had told him afterward that he was the luckiest man alive. If he had followed protocol and stopped to issue a mayday over the radio, he would have still been inside the apartment when the ceiling came down. But he had known better. It wasn't luck or breaking protocol that had saved him. Keeping calm and using logic were what kept him alive that day.

Now, he was nervous—and he couldn't control it. Logic told him they were making the right move taking Veronica to Jackson's condo in the Castro. But his gut was screaming that something was wrong with this situation. He didn't want to let on with Veronica and Cara until he had a better reason to change their plan than "firefighter intuition"—especially because this was all his idea.

The way he felt about Veronica was so new to him. He'd never felt like that about a woman before. That must be where his nerves were coming from. His runaway heart was making a mess of him. *That's all it is*, he thought as he guided George's old Honda off the Bay Bridge and into the city. *This thing with Veronica just has me all turned around is all.*

Twenty-Two

Veronica

Though at first Veronica hadn't liked the idea of talking to a journalist about what she found in Sunset's server room, she was grateful that Angus had talked her into it. For the first time since she found the bug on the hard drive, she was clear on what she had to do. After days on the run, feeling like she wasn't in control of any part of this situation, not knowing what the right move was from moment to moment...she liked that she could *do* something now. She could finally take action. She was no longer going where the wind blew her, or waiting for Sunset to make their next move. She was, for the first time since she got fired, in control.

"I'll pick you up in an hour," Cara said, hugging Veronica tight as they all stood on the wide sidewalk in front of the four-story apartment building. "I'm just going to go home and get cleaned up. Call me if you need *anything*."

Angus stood back, his hands tucked into the front pockets of his jeans. Veronica looked at him over Cara's shoulder. He looked...lost. Backlit by the setting sun, his shape was hunched and boyish, as if he was waiting to get sent to the principal's office.

"Thank you," Veronica said, squeezing Cara's shoulders as she pulled back. "I'll be okay." Her eyes drifted to Angus's downcast face.

Cara looked behind her and seemed to notice her brother for the first time. "I'm going to get out of here. I'll let you two say your goodbyes." As she walked by Angus on her way to her car parked down the block, she whispered something in his ear. Angus playfully punched her arm, and she punched him back, less playfully.

Veronica and Angus were alone on the sidewalk, the autumn light growing dimmer by the second.

"Thanks for..."

"I shouldn't have..."

They laughed as they talked over each other.

Veronica cleared her throat. "Thank you for...well, for everything. For saving my life, most importantly."

"You're welcome," Angus said with a half smile. "But I'd sleep a lot better tonight if you would let me walk you to Jackson's door."

Veronica shook her head. "You've done enough. You have a life you need to get back to." *Besides, I just want to get this over with.* She noticed that Angus seemed to shrink a little as she spoke. Reaching out her hand, she cupped his cheek and he leaned into the caress. "Will you call me?" she asked in a quiet voice. She instantly regretted asking that question. Encouraging a relationship with her best friend's brother was a royally bad idea.

Angus's brown eyes lit like sparklers. "Yes," he said. "Absolutely. I was hoping this weekend wasn't just...I don't know...a reaction to stress."

The implication cut Veronica like a knife. She removed her hand from his face and took a step back. "Oh, so you think I was turned on by being a damsel in distress?"

Angus's head snapped up and his chocolate eyes bored into hers. "You are anything but a damsel in distress. But in my line of work, I've seen some extreme reactions to stressful situations."

"So you sleep with all the women you've rescued, is that what you're saying?" Veronica seethed.

"No, of course not!" Angus stumbled back.

"I have to go," Veronica said with a backward glance at the white apartment building. "I'm sure Jackson is wondering what's keeping me." She winced when she turned back and saw the hurt on Angus's face. "The faster I can get Sunset off my back, the faster we can all get back to our normal lives." *And the faster you can move on and find a woman who isn't so much trouble.* Turning on her heel, she strode up to the glass door of the apartment building. As she grasped the handle, she stopped and turned back toward Angus. "Thank you. I mean that."

"You don't owe me any thanks. I mean that," he responded, his expression impossible for Veronica to read.

She entered the apartment building feeling a mix of guilt and fear. It wasn't a good combination for her nervous system. Veronica wasn't sure if she wanted to puke or faint. At least her nose wasn't throbbing anymore.

Taking the stairs two at a time, she made her way to the fourth floor, then crossed the carpeted hallway to apartment 4A. She paused with her knuckles ready to rap on the door. *Is this the right thing to do? What if talking to this journalist causes more problems?*

Veronica screwed up her courage and knocked loudly on the apartment door. The door swung open half an inch, but she heard no indication that someone was coming to answer her knock. "Hello?" she said loudly into the crack. Heart racing, she nudged the door open another inch and called out again. Still no one answered.

Carefully peering into the opening, she noticed a pile of books and papers scattered about the floor. Veronica leaned into the door and opened it enough to slip in.

At first the apartment just looked like it had been ransacked. Odds and ends were strewn all over the living room, and furniture was at odd angles. She smelled a familiar cologne just before she noticed the rivulet of blood streaming slowly across the pale wood floors from the kitchen into the living area.

Veronica rushed to the kitchen and found a man on the floor, blood rushing from a wound on his head. She dropped to her knees next to him and felt for a pulse. "Mr. Diaz?" His pulse was weak, but it was there. "Mr. Diaz, I'm calling for help." She reached for the purse she had dropped on the floor, and pulled out her phone.

Just as Veronica opened the phone app and began dialing 911, the sound of metal clicking against metal alerted her that she wasn't alone.

"I wouldn't do that if I were you, Veronica Clark," said a male voice from behind her.

She turned to see Sunset CEO Craig Truman holding a gun on her—and George was standing next to him.

VERONICA SAT NERVOUSLY ON THE EDGE OF THE COUCH as George rifled through her purse. The queasy, lightheaded feeling was gone, now, and her nerves were taut as guitar strings. It was always in these moments when she was facing a crisis alone that her head became clearest. No one else was going to rescue her or make decisions for her—she had to act.

She knew what she had to do, but she wanted information before she made her move.

"Why, George?" she said to the man she had once called friend. He looked like a stranger to her now. No longer moving in his absentminded, almost frail manner, he moved sharply and purposefully.

George's hawklike eyes took her in, and he sniffed with derision. "Do you think for a second I could retire comfortably on a government pension in California? I couldn't even afford a trailer home in Stockton, much less keep my home in Sausalito." He pulled the hard drive out of Veronica's purse and held it aloft. "It's deactivated, you know. And the drive is wiped. No one would have found anything."

"Then why give it back to me?" Veronica asked, squinting at George. "And why the ruse? Why send me out of town?"

"I gave you the hard drive so you wouldn't suspect me," George said with a shrug. "And I sent you out of town because it would be easier for these clowns to make your death look like an accident. Unfortunately, you were harder to track with the software bug implanted in your email app than I anticipated. And you were harder to kill than I anticipated, too. I had to put a stronger tracker on you."

"But someone left a voicemail demanding the hard drive when I was driving home from your house—when you already had it. None of this makes any sense." Veronica subtly scanned the room as she kept George talking. A heavy object, something sharp, a way to make noise...there had to be something she could use to get out of this.

"They didn't know I had it yet," George said. "What, do you think I just picked up the phone and called them? Everything digital and everything that flows through a wire is traceable. You know that better than most."

"Will you two quit yapping?" Craig snapped, waving the gun. "We've got the hard drive. Let's get this done." He leveled the gun at Veronica. His hand was shaking, but it was barely perceptible.

He's anxious, but not nervous, I think. He really is going to shoot me. Veronica swallowed hard.

"And what about you?" Veronica asked Craig. "What do you get out of all of this?"

"You never got it," Craig snarled. "You never understood what it was we did at Sunset. What do you think financial management is?"

Veronica raised an eyebrow. "Managing finances?"

"It's manipulating data. Money isn't real anymore, it's just a collection of data points. The more data we have, the more money we can make." A slow smile crept across his face. "You thought you were so smart. So much better than the rest of us paper pushers. You locked down our data so no one else could take it—but you didn't notice that we were giving some of it away freely in exchange for different data." His thumb slid up and down the handle of the gun, lazily stroking the weapon. "The world runs on money. Money runs on data. You, though, are done running."

Veronica could sense that Craig was about to end his argument with her once and for all. *What's the right move, Veronica? What do you do? You have one shot.* In a split second, she assessed the situation in her mind. Craig's gun had a longer barrel than her Glock. It looked like a .22 caliber pistol. It probably wouldn't kill her—as long as the bullet didn't directly hit her head or any major organs.

Craig widened his stance and aimed.

She had to take the chance.

Veronica launched herself off the couch and into Craig, knocking him sideways into George. Craig fired the gun as he fell, but the bullet hit the couch. While the men were off-center, she sprang to the kitchen and grabbed her phone off the floor next to Jackson Diaz's still unmoving body.

Before Craig and George could figure out what was happening, Veronica was out the door.

TWENTY-THREE
ANGUS

"I came to pick Veronica up from Jackson's apartment, and she isn't here, and the place is crawling with cops," Cara told Angus over the phone. Her words ran together, as they always did when she was panicking about something.

"Do you think maybe she took a ride-share home?" Angus asked as he flipped the burger he was grilling on his stove. The burger landed awkwardly on the edge of the pan, and he bit back a curse.

"Not without calling me. She doesn't flake like that. And she's not picking up her phone," Cara said, her voice shaking. "Wait. Wait, they're wheeling out a gurney. Angus, there's a sheet over whoever it is."

Angus's heart leaped into his throat. "Cara, I need you to take a deep breath and try to stay calm right now," he said, half to his sister and half to himself. "Look as closely as you can without getting in the way. Do you see any part of the body? A hand hanging down? Shoes sticking out?"

"No," Cara whimpered.

"See if you can get information from one of the uniforms. Tell them your friend was in the building, and she was supposed to meet you. They may take pity on a sweet face." Angus's stomach turned as he spoke. "I'm going to call Jackson. I'll call you back."

After he hung up, he turned off the stove and dialed Jackson's number as he walked back toward his bedroom to get dressed. Boxers and a t-shirt wouldn't do if he had to rush out the door.

Jackson's phone rang and rang. When it finally went to voicemail, it gave him an automated message that the mailbox was full.

This can't be happening. I shouldn't have let Veronica out of my sight until we were sure Sunset was off her back. He threw on jeans and a black sweater, then called Cara back.

"Any luck?" he asked her when she picked up.

"I don't think it's her," Cara said over the sounds of dozens of voices in the background. "No one will give me any information, but I've been eavesdropping. They keep referring to the person on the gurney as 'he.'"

"Oh thank God." Relief flooded Angus's body, and he all but collapsed on his bed.

"I'm going to head to Veronica's apartment," Cara said. The background noise grew quieter, and Angus guessed she must be walking away from Jackson's apartment building now.

He sat up. "I'll meet you there."

Angus and Cara knocked on Veronica's door and rang the doorbell for the third time. She obviously wasn't home.

Cara looked sideways at her brother. "I know where Veronica keeps the spare key."

"Get it," Angus said without hesitation.

Cara turned and strode to the end of the hall, where a small table sat with an oriental vase on it. She lifted the vase with one hand and felt under the bottom of it with the other. Slowly, she peeled off a piece of tape from the bottom of the vase. A key fell onto the table with a clang.

Angus scooped up the key and unlocked Veronica's door before any of the neighbors could investigate the sound.

Everything inside the apartment was exactly as they had left it Saturday morning.

"What the hell happened here?" Cara said as she stepped around Angus and took in the mess in the living room.

"Someone broke in when we took the hard drive to George in Sausalito."

Cara squinted. "A second break in?"

"Technically this was the third," he said with a shrug. "Now you know why we went to the cabin. And why we didn't want to involve you. These people are determined...and dangerous."

"You both should know better than to leave me out of the loop," Cara said with a frown. "About anything."

The emphasis she put on that last word made Angus's cheeks burn.

"I hope we can find her soon," Cara said as she took a seat on the couch.

With the glittering city lights out the window behind her, Angus thought his sister looked ethereal and the slightest bit angelic. He fought the urge to snicker, which would be wholly inappropriate at a time like this.

"Where else would Veronica go?" Angus asked, sitting in the blue wingback chair across from Cara.

She shrugged. "If the sun was up, I'd say we should check the beach. But this late in the evening, the only other place she'd go besides home would be to work." She yawned loudly, then shook her head as if to clear it. "And we both know she's not at work."

Angus watched his sister and noticed, with some chagrin, just how tired she was. "I think you should head home," he said. "I'll stay here, and I'll call you when she shows up." He tried to sound perkier than he felt. Without being able to reach Veronica on her cell, waiting at her apartment was the only thing to do—but it also felt like he was doing nothing by staying there.

"I'm so worried about her," Cara said, her eyes glistening with fatigue and unspilled tears. "I don't want to leave. But I'm exhausted after so much driving today, and I have to be at the school at the crack of dawn tomorrow." The tears began to fall. "I don't know what to do."

Angus moved to sit with his sister on the couch. He put his arm around her shoulders and pulled her into a hug. "Little sis, I'm telling you what to do, and you need to listen to me for once. Go home. Get some sleep. I will stay here and wait for Veronica." He felt Cara's sob, and he squeezed her a little tighter. "While I'm here, I will call the hospitals and police stations, and I will call you the second I get any information."

Cara nodded against his shoulder. "You have to promise me —*promise* me—that you won't keep me out of the loop anymore. Let me know what you know, when you know it." She looked up at Angus, her red-rimmed eyes filled with a mix of worry and anger.

"I promise," he said, wiping her tears away. "Go home and get some sleep."

ANGUS SLOWLY SAT UP ON THE COUCH WHERE HE'D fallen asleep, and groaned at the pain in his back. By 10 p.m., he had called every police station and hospital in San Francisco, one in Oakland, and one in Daly City. While he had been frustrated that he didn't know where she was, he had also been relieved to not have found her through those channels.

He had no idea when he had fallen asleep, but the ache in his mid-back told him he must have been down for a while. Picking the phone up off the floor, the glowing numbers confirmed his suspicion. The time was inching toward 1 a.m. *Where the hell is Veronica?*

Angus stood and stretched. His back cracked as he reached toward the ceiling, and again when he reached toward the floor. There was enough light coming in through the window from streetlamps, headlights, and insomniacs' windows that he didn't need to turn on any lights in Veronica's apartment to see. He walked around the coffee table and stepped up to the bay windows. Every once in a while, a car would rumble down the street or a dog would bark—but other than that, the world was quiet. The hazy San Francisco sky was lit from underneath by the shimmering city, keeping the stars hidden from view. When he closed his eyes and focused, he could make out the sound of a TV coming up through the vent at his feet.

Staring at the city beyond the glass, Angus felt heavy and worn. Guilt ate at him. His last conversation with Veronica had gone terribly. After everything they'd been through together, he should have done a better job expressing his care for her. Instead, he made her feel like she was a charity case—or worse, that she was just another girl he had a fling with. He didn't take the opportunity to tell her how special she was to him, and how she'd pulled him out of his selfish bubble. He didn't tell her how strong he thought she was, or how excited he was to learn everything there was to know about her.

Now, looking out at the city that had swallowed her whole, Angus wanted nothing but another chance.

Out of the corner of his eye, Angus caught movement across the street from the apartment house. He watched carefully as a human form darted from shadow to shadow. Suddenly, they ran across the fully lit street—and in the light of the streetlamps, he could finally see clearly who it was.

Veronica stood on the shadowed sidewalk in front of the Victorian apartment house and looked up at the window where Angus stood.

Angus watched in horror as a car drove up the road and slowed as it approached her. From his vantage point, he could see the window roll down, and the gun protrude from the opening.

He pounded on the glass of the bay window, but Veronica didn't move.

Running full-tilt across the apartment and out the door, Angus was halfway down the stairs when he heard the gunshots.

Twenty-Four
Veronica

Veronica had been running all night. Every shape and shadow appeared dangerous—and she didn't know what Sunset was tracking on her phone. Could they tell who she was calling? Could they listen in on her conversations? Could they track the apps she used? With George on their side, there was no telling what they could find out from this little device in her pocket.

So she walked—and ran. San Francisco, like most major cities, could be dangerous at night. It was also easy to navigate on foot. She kept vigilant, held her head up confidently, and thanked her strong legs for carrying her swiftly from the Castro to the San Francisco Chronicle office on Mission Street, and over to Nob Hill. Four miles wasn't far by normal standards, but tonight it may have well been a million miles. Every footstep felt like one step closer to death if Craig caught up with her.

Going home was risky. But she needed clean clothes, cash, and her spare laptop—and she knew she could grab that stuff and be out quickly. She just prayed that Cara wasn't there waiting for her.

As she crossed over to Taylor Street, her legs burned. She was in excellent shape from all the time she spent out on her surfboard, but the hills of San Francisco were challenging for the toughest physique.

She couldn't shake the feeling that she was being followed as she grew nearer to her apartment. Ducking between two row houses, she stood and listened for a moment. The sounds of traffic in the distance and the beating of her own heart were the only noises she could hear. She took some deep breaths to slow her pulse before stepping back out onto the sidewalk.

Her apartment house came into view. She slipped from shadow to shadow, trying to stay out of sight in case someone was waiting for her there.

When it looked safe, she crossed the street.

That's when she noticed a figure in the window of her apartment.

A split second later, she heard the sound of a car approaching. In the time it took to look down the road and back again at her apartment, the person in the window was gone.

The approaching car slowed and Veronica's heart raced. She bolted around the garage side of the house just as the first shot rang out. She heard two more shots before the fourth shot split the wood siding next to her head. She dropped to the ground.

Veronica sat huddled on the driveway, holding her hands over her ears as a cacophony assaulted her. Tires squealed. Dogs barked raucously from windows. Men shouted from open doorways. Metal crunched against metal.

Veronica felt a solid warmth next to her, and just as suddenly as the cyclone of noise began, the world quieted around her. She opened her eyes and took her hands away from her ears.

Angus was crouched down next to her. He was saying something, but she couldn't hear him. Her relief was so great, blood roared in her ears, and the world spun around the axis that was Angus.

Neighbors and policemen swarmed around them. Questions

came at them rapid-fire. "Is she hurt?" "What happened here?" "What direction did the shooter go?" "Do you know her?"

Veronica wrapped her arms around Angus's neck and finally felt calm in the eye of the storm. She pulled back and put her hands on either side of his face, feeling the stubble against her palms. Pulling him in, she kissed him deeply.

TWENTY-FIVE
ANGUS

ANGUS BREATHED IN THE SUNSCREEN AND ROSES SCENT of her as Veronica kissed him. "Are you okay?" he asked her between kisses, stroking her hair to check for head wounds.

Veronica nodded. "I didn't get hit."

Too soon, policemen and emergency personnel were all around, demanding their attention—and reluctantly, he pulled away.

A tall patrol officer stepped out of the crowd and toward Angus and Veronica. "Is this Veronica Clark? Sir, please step aside. I need to know if this is Veronica Clark." He spoke at Angus in rapid-fire succession.

Angus looked at the shaken, exhausted blonde.

Veronica gave him a barely perceptible nod, then answered the police officer. "Yes, I'm Veronica Clark."

The officer stepped closer to Veronica. "Jackson Diaz left instructions with his partner to check on you immediately if anything happened to him. I assume you know what happened to Diaz last night..."

"Yes," Veronica nodded shakily. "Is he going to be okay?"

Angus was relieved that Veronica didn't give any more detail than that. He didn't have all the details about what happened at Jackson's apartment, but when it came to dealing with the police after a crime, it was always better to stay silent until your lawyer got there.

The officer lowered his eyebrows. "He's in bad shape. But they say he'll live."

"That's a relief," Veronica said, putting a hand to her chest. She looked around, suddenly noticing all the activity around her. Two ambulances were parked on the side of the narrow street, while a firetruck took up both driving lanes. There were patrol cars in every driveway she could see from where she stood. "Did everyone here come to check on me?"

The officer snorted. "No, ma'am. People tend to call 911 when they hear gunshots." He smiled warmly. "Only my partner and I, and two other patrol officers, came to follow up on Diaz's message. Are you physically okay? Do you need an ambulance? Did you see who fired the gun?"

"I'm fine. And I didn't see the shooter. Just the car."

"It's probably best for the paramedics to look you over," the officer said, frowning.

Angus was getting irritated now. This beanpole was wasting time. "She said she's fine," he said, addressing the officer. "Did you catch the shooter?"

The officer didn't answer, but raised his eyebrows at Veronica.

"Really, I'm okay. Just shaken up," she said.

The officer frowned deeper, but nodded his assent. "They swerved and crashed into a dumpster just up the road. We got 'em."

"Oh thank God," Veronica said, leaning against the wall for support.

"If you're okay, I'm going to go help at the scene. Here's my card." The officer held out a card and Veronica took it. "I'm going to be in touch to get your statement." At that, he turned and walked swiftly into the fray.

Veronica took Angus's hand and bobbed her head toward the apartment house, motioning for him to follow.

Moments later they were holding each other tightly on Veronica's couch. The world dropped away. It was just Angus and Veronica in this bubble, and the whirl of activity on the street outside couldn't touch them.

"I shouldn't have left you alone," Angus said as he kissed her neck.

"I didn't give you a choice. I'm sorry I was so horrible. I got scared...scared of hurting you, scared of letting Cara down..." Veronica pulled back and let her head drop.

"It's okay. The only thing that matters is that you're all right. Everything else, we'll figure it out." Angus grinned. "I mean, clearly we make a good team."

Veronica stroked his cheek. "You'll give me another chance, then?"

Angus kissed her lips gently, then rested his forehead on hers. "You don't need a second chance. You never lost the first one."

TWENTY-SIX
VERONICA

"THE MULTINATIONAL CONSPIRACY STRETCHED FROM Beijing to San Francisco. Wealth managers traded insider tips and customers' confidential financial information over a secret network. Who knows how long it would have gone undiscovered if it weren't for the actions of one brave information security employee." On the TV screen above the long counter that ran the length of the 1950s-style diner, the cameraman panned from the reporter to the entrance of Sunset Financial Tower.

Angus waved his hand at the waitress as she passed. "Could you change the channel, please?" The story was on every news station, and every newscaster was saying the same thing.

Veronica sat between Cara and Angus at the counter. She had spent all of Monday at the police station, helping them sort out the details of the Sunset case. That night, she was so exhausted, she could barely manage to tell Cara the basics of what had happened. Only a promise of further conversation over pie and coffee before the school day began on Tuesday was enough to get Cara off the phone so she could get some sleep.

Angus had insisted on joining them at the diner. Veronica was grateful for the extra time with him, though she knew he only took the day off because he had an appointment at the police station to go over his involvement in what happened.

"So it wasn't espionage or corporate sabotage?" Cara asked between bites of peach pie.

"Nope. Just good old-fashioned insider trading and theft," Veronica answered, sipping her coffee.

"And they believed you, even without the hard drive."

"Thanks to Jackson and his colleague Elena at the Chronicle, yeah. They'd been investigating Sunset for months. My story was enough for them to finally be able to call in the cops."

"What did Craig have to say when he was arrested?"

"From what Angus's friend at the SFPD tells us, he pled the fifth. They found the gun under the front seat of his car, and the cops think it'll be a slam dunk to match it to the bullets they found at my apartment." Veronica sighed and sipped her coffee. "I would have loved to have been there to see the bastard in handcuffs."

Cara frowned. "And your friend George?"

"Not my friend," Veronica corrected. "Not since he started taking payments from Sunset." She sipped her black coffee and winced. Normally she didn't need sugar in her coffee, but this diner made one strong cup of joe. "They found George on a BART train in Milpitas. They think he was headed toward the Mexico border."

Angus snorted. "All that work to keep his house in Sausalito, and he would have spent his remaining days in Tijuana." He took a big bite of his breakfast sandwich and shook his head at the TV, which was now tuned into a fishing show.

"I'm still confused why George would bring you the hard drive," Cara said, ignoring her brother.

"He bugged my phone," Veronica said, taking her phone off the counter and wiggling it at Cara.

Cara nearly choked on her pie. "How did he manage..."

"It was so small and discreet I didn't notice it until yesterday when I was thinking how Sunset always seemed to be one step ahead of me. When I took a close look at my phone case, I saw it—a tiny little bug right near the camera lens. George must have stuck it on when he handed me my phone in Truckee."

"When he was faking being shot."

"Exactly."

"Clever old man."

Veronica shrugged. "Desperate, more like it. It's one more piece of evidence against him and Sunset now."

"Hey you two," Angus said loudly, giving Cara a sharp jab in the ribs. "Look." He pointed at the TV with his sandwich.

Cara elbowed him back as all three of them looked to see what was important enough to interrupt the fishing show.

Two news anchors sat at a curved desk. The woman on the right, dark haired and serious, tapped a stack of paper as a baritone voice introduced the special report.

The news anchor on the left, a pert blonde, spoke. "This just in. Craig Truman, CEO of recently scandalized Sunset Financial, was killed in a drive-by shooting one hour ago."

A lump rose in Veronica's throat.

The blonde anchor continued, "Police were escorting Mr. Truman into the courthouse when a black Dodge Charger pulled up and the passenger opened fire. Mr. Truman was killed instantly. Police are asking anyone with information to come forward. Again, the vehicle was a black Dodge Charger, and the license plate number begins with XY5."

"Holy crap," Angus said, setting what remained of his sandwich back on the plate. He turned to Veronica. "What does this mean?"

"It means that Craig pissed off some very dangerous people," Veronica said. The lump in her throat was beginning to feel more like a jagged stone.

Cara put her hand on Veronica's shoulder. "Could they be coming for you, too?"

"I don't know," Veronica said. "I don't know."

LATER THAT AFTERNOON, VERONICA MULLED OVER THE news as she floated on her board in the frigid ocean off the coast of San Francisco. Unlike the San Francisco Bay, the Pacific Ocean was raw and unprotected. The waves here churned and spat, pricking her with icy fingers. It wasn't a great place to float mindlessly—but the larger, wilder waves offered the distraction she had been craving since she found out Craig had been killed.

She licked the salt from her chapped lips and squinted at the sun as it ducked behind a large cloud. The air smelled of brine and seaweed. Running her fingers to and fro over the smooth surface of her board, she listened to the distant sound of seagulls and contemplated her next move.

Only a few other surfers were out in the water that afternoon, and there was no competition for waves. Unfortunately, there weren't many waves to choose from. Winter would bring larger swells, but the water that day just felt cold and lonely. Her flesh prickled with goosebumps under her wetsuit, and even the gentle rocking of her board couldn't soothe her.

Maybe it's time to head in. She leaned down and paddled with her right hand to turn her board toward the faraway beach. A few people-shaped figures dotted the sand, some sitting in chairs and others walking the waterline. One figure stood still and alone, and seemed to be looking at her.

Veronica laid belly-down on her board and began paddling toward land.

TWENTY-SEVEN
ANGUS

ANGUS WAS MESMERIZED WATCHING VERONICA MOVE through the deep blue-gray water on her surfboard. As smooth and confident as she was on land, she was infinitely so in the water. He waved at her as soon as she was close enough, and she raised one dripping wet hand to wave back.

Veronica paddled her board as far as she could, then hopped off and walked the rest of the way through the white foam with the turquoise board tucked under her arm. Her wetsuit glistened with saltwater, and her blonde braid dripped as she pulled it over her shoulder and squeezed out the water.

"You found me," Veronica said with a smile as she met Angus on the beach. "Shouldn't you be at the police station?"

"I was—that's how I heard the news before it hit the media." Angus put his arm around Veronica and began to nudge her ever so gently toward the parking lot.

"News...what news?" she asked.

"Jackson woke up from his coma, and he was able to point the police to the people on the other end of the Sunset scheme."

"You mean, the company they were exchanging insider information with in another country?"

"It wasn't a company."

Veronica's eyes widened and she swallowed hard.

"It was an organized crime syndicate."

Veronica reached across and put her hand on Angus's chest, stopping their forward motion. "What does this mean?" she asked, her teeth beginning to chatter.

Angus shrugged. "It means that George wasn't lying when he said it was so much bigger than we thought it was. It could mean that because the cat's out of the proverbial bag, you're not a target anymore. Or it could mean an international mafia will want revenge on the woman who stumbled on their secret network." He tightened his arm around Veronica's wet shoulders, willing the heat of his body to warm her up as they stood on the windy beach near the steps leading up to the parking area.

"I'm not running this time," she said without a flicker of hesitation in her voice. Her shoulders squared as she locked eyes with Angus.

"I was hoping you'd say that," he said with a grin.

Veronica cocked an eyebrow at him.

"As soon as I heard that Jackson had woken up, I headed to the hospital. To say he's furious about how things went down would be an understatement. He wants to pick the story back up and write up a full account—and he wants your help."

"How can I help a reporter?"

"He wants you to consult on the story, help him understand and explain the technical aspects of what Sunset was doing with the secret network."

Veronica's lips pressed together as she processed the new information—but it took her only seconds to come to an answer. "I'm in." She tilted her head and looked at Angus with her Pacific blue eyes. "Maybe this is the beginning of a brand new career as a consultant." She smiled from ear to ear. "I'll wear jeans to the office and take afternoons off to surf. I like being self-employed already."

EPILOGUE
ANGUS

"Can we have a table at the back? Away from the windows, please." Angus spoke to the hostess at Restaurant 415, but his eyes were scanning the room.

"You know, the police don't think I'm a target," Veronica whispered, pulling on his elbow.

"No, they said to be careful and report anything suspicious. I'm not taking any chances," he replied quietly as the hostess checked the seating chart.

The young brunette hostess squinted her eyes at them. "I can seat you at table 23, near the kitchen. Is that okay?"

Angus stretched his neck to see where the kitchen door was, then he nodded at the young woman. "Perfect."

Angus held Veronica's hand tight as the hostess led them through the busy restaurant. When they reached the small, candlelit table, he pulled out Veronica's chair. She gave him a warm smile and took her seat.

"This is nice," she said when the hostess was gone. Opening up her paper menu, she tapped it with her index finger. "They have salmon. I already know what I want."

"I thought it was about time for our first date," Angus said. He smiled at the confused look Veronica gave him over the top of her menu.

"We've been dating for months," she said, putting the menu down and sipping her water. "I mean, unless you have another name for what we've been doing." She winked at him. "It's probably bad manners to say those things in polite company, though."

Angus felt the heat rise from his neck to his cheeks, and shook his head. "No, I mean a proper date. We've never really had a proper date. We've been running from one danger or another since the moment we met. I thought it was time to take a moment and... be normal."

Veronica frowned. "You don't think I'm normal?"

"I think you're extraordinary," he countered.

She laughed. "Good answer."

A server approached their table holding a bottle of wine in one hand and a corkscrew in the other. "The Pinot Grigio you ordered, sir?"

"We just sat down, I haven't looked at the wine menu..." Veronica started.

Angus waved his hand at the server. "Yes, thank you."

Veronica shot a befuddled look at Angus across the table, but didn't argue.

The server reached across the table and filled Veronica's wine glass a quarter of the way, then did the same for Angus before putting the bottle down on the table. "Good evening," he said as he turned and left.

"That was odd," Veronica said. "In fact, I'd say that was downright suspicious." She squinted at her glass.

"Nonsense," Angus said, raising his glass. "Let's toast to a normal date."

"Okay..." Veronica said slowly, raising her glass to Angus's. In the light of the candle, she finally noticed what was in the bottom of the glass.

Angus's heart leapt in his chest.

"Is that..." she said as she reached into the glass with her index finger. "...A ring?" She held out the slim gold band with a half-carat diamond perched on it.

Angus knelt next to the table and took her free hand in his. "Veronica Constance Clark, these last few months with you have been the best months of my life. I can't imagine going another day without your wit, your strength, your beauty...and your talent for making a fantastic cup of coffee," Angus said with a sly grin. "I want to hold you close, to support your dreams, and to keep you safe for the rest of my life. Will you do me the honor of marrying me?"

Veronica stared at him while an older couple nearby clapped warmly. She looked around, seemingly overwhelmed.

Just when Angus started doubting, Veronica slipped from her chair and knelt down next to him. She fixed her intense blue eyes on his face, squeezed his hand, and finally replied. "Yes. Nothing would make me happier."

In that one moment, an entire, beautiful life together filled his mind's eye. He didn't know what the future held, but one thing he knew for certain—he would spend it with Veronica.

Please Review

We hope that you've enjoyed *Firewall*
by Jessica Mehring.
Please consider leaving a review for this title.

Please rate and review : *Firewall*

MEET THE AUTHOR

Jessica Mehring is a Colorado-based author, copywriter and consultant. She believes that history and nature are our greatest teachers, yet she is also endlessly fascinated by technology and the human brain. She loves reading, walks in the woods, and creating and collecting art. She lives with her husband, two daughters, and more pets than she'd like to admit to—and her growing collection of books and office supplies are slowly taking over their house.

You can connect with Jessica at jessicamehringauthor.com.

OTHER TITLES FROM

5 PRINCE PUBLISHING